WINDOW DRESSING

JODI PAYNE
BA TORTUGA

Published by Tygerseye Publishing, LLC
December 2019
Printed in the USA

To our wives

PROLOGUE

Sterling Kingsolver was fixin' to ruin his goddamn career for stupid pride, and he gave less than no shits.

He stood there, staring at Clint Masterson, the buzz of fury zipping between his ears like killer bees.

"Listen to me, boy. Cody Ball has been promised this year. You're a baby. You're a rookie. You throw this ride and we'll make it worth your while."

"I ain't a cheat." He might be a piece-of-shit caliche farmer, a desert baby balls to bones, but he wasn't about to take a dive. He had Rookie of the Year in the bag, sure—but if he rode his last bull? Shit marthy, he would take the event win and the championship.

"We aren't asking you to cheat, son. I'm telling you to make a smart career move, hmm?" Masterson had been one of the First Five, and he was the face of the league, the big boss. Shit, this man could ruin him. Shit.

"Fine. I think it's bullshit, man. Total bullshit." God. God help him. Was he considering this?

"This isn't some little ranch rodeo, Kingsolver. This is the big time. Sometimes you have to lose a little. You got the

Rookie of the Year money. Take it and run. Next year it will be yours."

Right. Assuming he stayed healthy next year. Assuming he rode. Assuming he had another magic year. "Yessir."

Fucker.

"Good boy. Go on. You need to strap in. Don't make it obvious."

Good boy?

Good fucking boy?

He stormed across the chutes, his boots rattling.

"Bit! Bit, come on! Tie on your damn glove! This is it." Jack waved and bounced, his eyes as big as saucers. "What did Masterson want?"

"Nothing. Just to keep my ass on the bull."

"Ah. Okay. Grab your bull rope. I'll pull. Chance can hold your vest."

"Right." He went through the motions, acidic hatred burning in his belly. Motherfuckers, with their politics and shit. He could see Cody Ball and his long-assed ugly nose and sparse pussy-tickler mustache just staring him down with a bullshit smirk, knowing what they'd asked.

Just because Ball hadn't fucking managed quite to keep himself centered, just because no one had thought Sterling was a goddamn threat until it was too late.

Now he was one ride away from taking the whole thing.

One ride.

His daddy was sitting there in the stands, the day sheet crumpled in his fingers. Daddy would know. He would know and judge, even if he never said a word about it.

"Focus, asshole!" Chance shook him. "Blue Belly isn't going to thank you for woolgathering." His old friend leaned close, peppermint on his breath. "Don't do it. Ride this son of a bitch. Ride him into the motherfucking ground and make them all scream."

"They said—"

"Don't. Just hold on, cowboy. You ain't a rodeo athlete; you're a goddamn cowboy."

Sterling nodded and got his legs set, slamming his glove shut over his rope. Blue Belly bucked in the chute, tossing his head, slamming Sterling's leg against the gate. He didn't nod, but the gate swung open, and he kept his mind in the middle.

Just hold on. *You're a goddamn cowboy.*

That was right. He was. He was a goddamn cowboy, and he didn't throw rides. This wasn't a job; this was who he was.

By the time he finished telling himself that, the buzzer sounded, the arena going wild.

Well, okay then.

Time to hit the dirt and take his lumps.

1

Jonas Burke walked into the office on a freezing cold Friday morning with a tray of Starbucks lattes in one hand and his cell phone in the other, consulting Quora about the best place to go dancing in Curaçao.

He might have been skipping, if not for the hot coffees in his hand. Tomorrow he'd be far away from the frozen streets of New York City and on the beach by lunchtime, stretched out in a chaise, with a cold adult beverage, wearing sunglasses and covered in coconut-scented sunscreen.

"Morning, Jonas."

"Morning, baby." He flashed Mia his brightest smile. "I brought you a latte!"

Mia loved her lattes, but she was too smart for the bribery game. Who was he kidding?

She smiled at him. "Oh, you do love me. Or... wait a minute." She eyed him. "You're going on vacation, aren't you?"

"I am. Seven days of fun in the sun." He couldn't wait. He'd been looking forward to his vacation for weeks. It was so damn cold and gray in New York.

"So this is... okay. Who am I stuck with?"

"Just Lulu and Archie. Gotta run. Love you!"

"Jonas!" Mia called after him. "Dammit, Jonas! It's the holidays!"

"Lalala, I can't hear you!" Next week was the week between Christmas and New Year's, that was true. But he almost always went away that week because it was typically quiet. Lulu and Archie were simple as far as clients went. They were both so predictable they were almost a waste of his celebrity-wrangling talent. He could juggle them both in one hand and calmly drink his latte with the other.

One of the remaining coffees was for him, and the last one was for—

"Jonas. You got a minute?"

Sid.

You weren't supposed to have a crush on the boss, he knew that, but he'd read that memo and burned it, sacrificing it to the Gods of Rule Followers. Sid McCann was a tall, blond Adonis of a man, and as wrong as it was—so wrong—Jonas could totally see them doing wonderfully dirty things together.

"For you? Always." He smiled and handed Sid a latte.

"A latte. Thank you. Come and sit?"

Oh. Oh, that sounded bad.

He went over the last few days in his head, trying to remember if he'd forgotten something or dropped the ball somehow. He wasn't being fired, was he?

Shit, if Sid fired him today, there'd be no way he could afford this vacation. He was going to be eating ramen for two weeks when he got back, as it was. He sat with a sigh.

"What's up, Sid?"

"Did you get travel insurance?"

"Of course. I always do." Hell yeah, he had. He couldn't

afford to lose the money on the trip if he had to cancel for work. He never knew when one of his clients was going to get a wild hair up their butt and suddenly need him to... oh.

Oh, come on. Really?

Shit.

He leaned back in his chair as his plans for the beach dissolved in an instant. "Which one of them is canceling my vacation? Is it Lulu again? For what, another award show?" *Dammit.* He should know better than to try to travel at the holidays.

"A VIP. I got a call from the, uh—" Sid shuffled some papers around on his desk and read the name. "—the WLBR. Stands for the Western League of Bull Riders. They need someone to wrangle their newest champion bull rider while he's in the city to do some publicity. I don't know much about bull riding, or the rodeo either, for that matter, but they tell me that in their world this cowboy is as big a celebrity as they come."

"You want me to work for a cowboy?"

"They called him a 'rodeo athlete.' And no. They want you to handle the cowboy. You'll be working for the league while he's in New York, getting him ready for photo shoots, prepping him for interviews, making sure he is where he is supposed to be when he—"

"Babysitting."

"Basically."

"Sid, that's entry-level PA stuff. Anyone can do that. We talked about getting me a leg up. I need a big client." And he could be on the beach.

"Apparently not anyone. The guy I spoke to says this cowboy is a rookie—a newbie at the PR stuff—and a little difficult. They've asked for someone with a lot of experience. And a backbone. You're that guy."

Was that a compliment? He wasn't sure. He wondered sometimes if he did his job *too* well. "So, you want me to give up seven days in the sun to make sure this Rhinestone Cowboy shows up shaved and on time to smile for the camera."

Sid didn't even crack a smile. "He's flying in sometime over the weekend. You'll start whenever they call you. Saturday night or Sunday, I'd assume. He's got a shoot first thing Monday morning. He'll be your only client for a bit because he's only here short-term, and you can take your vacation when he's done in town. They said it wouldn't be more than a week."

He sighed. "It's gotta be me?"

"You drew the short straw." Sid grinned at him. "Thanks for the coffee."

He got up, already rearranging his thinking, getting out of vacation mode, figuring out where to start with researching how one grooms a celebrity cowboy. He needed to research wardrobe and hairstyles, look at the magazines and YouTube and learn what he was in for. Hopefully the WLBR had a good budget. If he had to stay in a hotel, it better be a nice hotel.

"No problem," Jonas said, distracted, as he left the office.

"Jonas," Sid called out after him. "His name is Kingsolver. Sterling Kingsolver."

2

Sterling stepped out of security with his carry-on and his phone, not sure what the fuck he was supposed to do.

"Someone will meet you," Masterson had snarled. The "asshole" had been implied. This time.

Someone will meet you.

Shit.

Someone was fixin' to meet him to get his picture taken and talk to more damn cameras before he went home. He wasn't sure about what to expect. Masterson sure as shit wasn't going to share any information that he didn't have to. Just go, deal, smile.

"Mister Kingsolver?" A voice off to his left called his name again. "Sterling Kingsolver?" He looked over to find a dark-haired guy jogging toward him, flashing him a big smile full of bright white teeth.

"Yessir?" Lord, that man had a mouth like Luke Bryan.

"I thought that might be you. The hat and everything. I'm Jonas Burke. The uh... your league sent me." Burke stuck out a hand. "How was your flight?"

"I slept." All the folks around him were doing a grand job of trying to convince each other they were doing very important shit. Him? He was going to snooze and possibly pretend to snore.

"Well, that's good. We have a big day. You're only in town for a week, and your first interview is tomorrow, so we don't have a second to waste. Do you have luggage?" Burke started leading him through the airport, moving quickly, like they were late for something. "I've got a car waiting for us."

"I don't." Sterling knew how to use an iron, didn't he? Hell yes.

Burke looked him up and down. "Well, all right. Good thing we're going shopping. Guess I've got my work cut out for me."

Sterling got another grin, and then the guy dragged him through a revolving door. They popped out on a busy sidewalk, where there were suitcases, black cars, and yellow cabs lined up everywhere.

And it was fucking freezing cold.

"Over here, Mister Kingsolver."

A driver opened up the back door to a huge black sedan for them. "Can I put your bag in the trunk?" the guy asked, breath a visible cloud in the cold December air.

"I'm cool, thanks." He held one hand out to the driver. "Sterling. Pleased to meet you."

He didn't like getting into a car with a guy whose name he didn't know.

The driver shook, looking surprised. "Uh. I'm Louis, sir. Have a seat."

Burke let himself in on the other side and made a phone call as soon as the car started to move.

"Hey, it's me. I've got Mister Kingsolver. We're going to hit a few places for wardrobe. Can I just have everything sent over to the hotel? Perfect. He'll need to freshen up when we check in, and...." Burke looked him over again. "And we'll clean him up a bit. I'll text you when I get him to his room. Yeah. Got it. Thanks."

Sterling texted Chance. *In NYC in a fancy assed car with Luke Bryan's teeth. Traffic looks like Austin and Houston had a baby.*

Burke blew into his fingers to warm them and pulled up a calendar on his phone. "The shoot is early tomorrow, so you'll want to get your beauty sleep tonight. I have a barber coming to the hotel later. Even with the fittings, you should have time to get a shower first. Sound good?"

Ha! Also creepy. You got something to keep them in? The teeth?

Sterling rolled his eyes but had to grin. Had to, even as he typed, *Fucker.*

Hope you got sunglasses. Chance's reply was followed by a thumbs-up.

Just following your advice on holding on, buddy. Wait. What? "Barber?"

He'd just got his hair cut last week.

"Sweet, yeah?" Burke looked to be flipping through emails and didn't look at him. "Right in your hotel room. We'll get you a shave and a trim, and then we can look at a couple of styles, see what works. Are you hungry? I can have food brought in too."

"Styles." He didn't have enough hair to do a style, did he? "You're awful perky for... whatever damn time it is."

Burke leaned forward and lifted a handle between the seats, opened up a cooler, and handed him a Starbucks Doubleshot. "It's about two o'clock. You must have hopped a dawn flight, huh?"

Felt like... shit, he didn't know. He'd slept hard, and now he was all stupid. "Yeah, I did."

Also, caffeine. Yay.

"Do you have green room requests for tomorrow? I'll need to let them know tonight."

"What?" He wasn't sure why anyone wanted to talk to the likes of him, anyway.

Burke's head snapped around, and the guy stared at him for a long moment looking... shocked? Worried? Whatever it was, Burke didn't seem happy about it. "Jesus. You're more of a newbie than I thought."

Do not reach out and pop this dude's head off like a pimple. Do not. Ain't his fault you got no idea what's what yet. "I just want to get settled and take a shower. You got a list of what all y'all need me to do?"

"I... a list? No, I don't have a list. We're starting with a couple of fitting appointments, though. Most people I work with don't have time to deal with more than a day ahead and just let me handle things. But if you'd like me to make you a schedule, I can—oh, hang on." Burke reached for his hand and cradled his fingers in a warm palm. "You need a manicure too."

"A manicure? Ain't they for girls?" Lord have mercy, the guys would ride him like a prized pony if they heard about that. "I got me a nail brush."

Momma had made sure of it.

"No, Mister Kingsolver... Sterling. Can I call you Sterling? Call me Jonas. Manicures are not just for women. They're also for very manly rodeo celebrity cowboys with ragged nails and deep, dry cuticles. That stuff doesn't look good on camera." Burke... Jonas patted his hand and flashed him another toothy smile, practically blinding him. "Don't worry, I won't tell your crew. I'll just text Mia. Get her manicurist to come over." Jonas started texting madly, thumbs flying.

He didn't even know what a deep cuticle was. He looked at his hands; they looked just fine. Normal.

"I got an email from the WLBR. They say tomorrow's shoot starts with you, but then they've got a handful of other guys coming in also. Have you done any of this before? Like, back in New Mexico? Or on the... what do you call it? Bull riding circuit? I mean, interviews and shoots? At all?"

Umbers. Oh, that was all bad. He knew Cody Ball would be on that list. He knew it. Cody came from big money in the Carolinas and hated him with the fiery passion of a thousand suns. If it was Cody and his gang.... Damn.

Oh, Mr. Teeth was waiting on him to answer. What was the question? Right. Had he done this? Fuck no.

"I'm a rookie. I just ride, huh?"

Jonas took a deep breath and sighed, like Sterling had just become a great, heavy ring around the man's neck. "All right. We'll do a mock interview. That will help. You need to have answered the big questions before like... uh. Wow rodeo questions. I don't know a damn thing about bull riding, to be honest, but... uh. Okay. How did you get into riding bulls? How old were you when you started?"

"I got on my first calf when I was five. A dare from my cousin Maria. She told me I wouldn't fall off if I rode him backassward and held on to his tail." She'd lied like whoa.

Jonas made a face. "Uh. How about the next time?"

"I reckon it was after the cast came off...."

"Okay, cowboy. Do me a favor. Close your eyes." Jonas shot him a look. "I know. Just go with it, will you? Close your eyes."

Weird. He closed his eyes, feeling about as stupid as anything.

Jonas patted his knee. "Good. Okay. It's like meditating, right? Creative visualization? You ever... no, never mind. That's a dumb question. So... think about why you ride. Think about... um. How it feels. Really think about it, you know? Think about what it felt like to win."

His grin just bloomed right on his face. He remembered his daddy right there, tears on his cheeks. He remembered Chance—*you're a goddamn cowboy.*

"Oh. Oh, cool! Look at you smiling. Okay. Um... now. Tell me about the first time you were on a bull. Just whatever comes to mind."

"Mira, look. I was riding at my first real event out near Shiprock, and it blew up a cloud. I mean, literally. The sky opened up, and it poured down, that bull spinning around, water flying off us." He'd landed facedown in the dirt, just *sploot.*

"Whoa. Did you win? Or, uh... you know. Do the eight-second thing? Did you make it?"

"I didn't. I bucked off at six point eight, but it was all fun, man." So much fun.

"Okay, good. See? That's your answer. When they ask you about how you got into riding, you tell them that story."

He started to open his eyes, and Jonas quickly covered them again. The man's fingers were warm, soft.

"Nope! Nope. Keep them closed. Now, tell me... tell me what you love about bull riding."

"It's all fast, no? And I have good friends, and I get to go and see places, but mostly it's a rush." He'd never have that otherwise. Hell, he'd taken Daddy to Denver to see him win the whole thing.

"And how did it feel to win in Denver? What was that moment like?"

"I felt like a goddamn cowboy."

"Well, yeah. Sure. But how did it feel?"

"We're here, Jonas."

"Thanks, Louis. Just... hang on a minute."

"It felt right." This was in his DNA. He wasn't an athlete; he was a cowboy.

"Well, I think you should come up with some better adjectives maybe, you know? Exhilarating or proud or vindicated? Maybe? But we got somewhere. You can open your eyes now. Louis, I'll text you when we're ready for stop number two."

"Yes, sir."

He opened his eyes just in time to see Jonas slide out of the car. He got his bag and nodded to the driver. "Thanks, Louis."

Then he got out and followed Mr. Teeth.

3

Jonas watched Sterling get out of the car with what essentially amounted to a backpack, and tried not to panic about his state of employment.

Seriously. What the actual fuck was he supposed to do with this clueless newbie in a cowboy hat? And a tiny clueless newbie at that. He hoped to hell the league knew what they were doing when they sent their wardrobe requests because he was nervous about what these Western outfitter places were going to come up with. Thankfully this was still New York, and the tailors and personal shoppers would speak his language. He was pretty damn sure Sterling had exactly nothing appropriate for an interview in that carry-on.

He'd better pay close attention because he couldn't afford to lose this job. Before this he'd been a paid-by-the-hour PA, fetching coffee and getting rich people's shoes shined and dogs groomed. Boring, menial shit that barely paid for subway fare, let alone neat things like food and rent. Jobs like this one were in high demand—hard to get and harder to keep. He wasn't about to let this cowboy from east bumfuck screw this up for him.

Talk about hillbilly—worn-out jeans, a plaid shirt, POS boots that probably had cow shit on them, and a hat that was listing to the left. This man was... God, did Sterling have all his teeth?

Okay. Never mind all of that. He had one job to do. Clean the cowboy up and make him camera ready. The better Sterling looked, the better he would look, and the better his next job would be. He took a deep breath and focused.

When Jonas was done with this cowboy, Sterling was going to shine from his newly whitened teeth to his silver belt buckle, to his brand-spanking-new boots.

They walked into the first store, and a salesperson came right over to Sterling. "Hey there, cowboy. Can I help?"

"We have an appointment," Jonas said casually.

"Oh. Are you Mister Burke? Great. We picked out a rack of things to start with, and Emily will be assisting you. Come with me?"

He heard a whispered "Assisting? The fuck?"

Do not roll your eyes. He's new at this. He's just... new.

They moved toward the back of the store and were shown into a large dressing room that had a rack along one wall of all kinds of clothing. Shirts and jeans and vests, all brand-new and fancy.

"I'll get Emily for you, and she'll help with your fitting. Can I get you some water or anything?"

"Sterling? Thirsty?"

"Yessir. Thank you. Water." Sterling gawked at the clothes. "It's like a Boot Barn in here."

He shrugged. He didn't know what a boot barn was.

"They have more than boots, obviously." He looked over the clothing, most of which seemed like it would do very nicely.

Thank God.

"Hi. I'm Emily. I brought you some water." Ah. Now, this he could work with. Emily was a petite, short-haired woman in all black. Not a stitch of cowgirl on her. "I know you're on a deadline, so why don't we start with the jeans, and then we can see what works from there?"

"Ma'am." Sterling tipped his hat and offered her a smile. Oh, look. He did have all his teeth. And, to be honest, that smile was kind of charming.

Emily smiled back. "Let's have a look." She walked in a circle around Sterling, and it was hard to tell if she was really sizing up the cowboy or ogling Sterling's ass. "Off with those, please." She pulled a pair of jeans from the rack and took them off the hanger.

Those dark eyes went wide. "Pardon? I ain't stripping down in front of a lady, ma'am."

Emily grinned at Sterling. "Well. Good thing I'm not a lady, then, cowboy. Hand them over."

Jonas snorted out a laugh. Oh, he liked this one. "We're all friends here, Sterling."

"Y'all got a weird idea of friends." Sterling blinked at Jonas, stared. "You're serious?"

"She's serious."

"Yep. I'm serious." Emily didn't sound like she was playing a bit. "Jeans, please."

Sterling sat down and tugged off his boots, then stood and unfastened his belt. All it took was the weight of the buckle to drag those jeans down.

"Pull these on. They're raw denim. I think you have the ass to pull them off. We got your measurements from your employer, so they should work. If not, I'll take some of my own." Emily handed them over.

"Can you just look away a little?"

"Why? Your boxer briefs are clean, aren't they?"

Sterling looked at Emily like she'd grown a second head, and then that upper lip curled, and Sterling went from embarrassed to icy cold. "Yes, ma'am, I can take them off and let you smell of them if you'd like."

Jonas physically covered his mouth to keep from laughing out loud.

"Not my kink, cowboy." But Emily turned her back, didn't she? Sterling: one, New York City: zero. He had to admire the man's tenacity.

"What's raw denim?"

"It hasn't been washed or preshrunk." Emily spoke over her shoulder while Sterling changed. "So when Mister Kingsolver wears them, they'll form to his shape and be super comfy. And they'll look great."

"Super comfy is good with me." Sterling stripped down, exposing legs without a hint of extra flesh—it was all tanned skin and scars.

Mm. Nice tan. He kept his eyes on Sterling's jeans. He wasn't trying to catch a look at cowboy ass, but he wasn't exactly not trying either.

As it turned out, the jeans were huge—Sterling was swimming in them.

"I thought you had measurements!" Jonas asked, so thankful that they hadn't just trusted the right things would show up at the hotel.

"We do, but apparently something got lost in translation to Yankee. Jesus. Take those off, Mister Kingsolver. I'm so sorry. I'll just take my own." Emily reached into her pocket and pulled out a tailor's tape measure and a small pad.

"You lose a lot of weight to compete...." Sterling watched Emily. "I wear a twenty-four."

Emily snorted and gave him the side-eye. "Inseam?"

"Thirty." Sterling stuck his tongue out at her.

She grinned and laughed, patting Sterling's shoulder as she walked past him. "You're all right, cowboy. I'll be right back."

For his part, Jonas was enjoying every second of this. "How much weight do you have to lose?"

"I lost damn near twenty-five since I went pro."

Twenty-five pounds? Was that healthy? "You're not competing now. You won the championship! You need a fucking cheeseburger, man."

"Oh...."

That sound was pure sex. Seriously. This kid was starving.

"Okay, Mister Kingsolver. Try these." Emily came breezing back into the dressing room, so Jonas added cheeseburgers to his to-do list for later. "A pair of raw and also a really nice pair of stonewashed that I just happen to like." She handed the jeans off to Sterling and dutifully turned her back. "Let me know what you think."

The stonewashed ones were dismissed out of hand, but the others were tried, doing wonders for Sterling's ass. "They fit okay, a little tight. Don't y'all just have some Wranglers?"

"Those are Wranglers. You're just not used to the raw, huh? You want to come look?"

Oh Jesus Christ. Let's not open that can of worms.

"Hold on." Jonas took a step toward Sterling. "Look. I don't care what brand you wear, but they need to be sharp, Sterling. They need to carry a price tag, you know? You just won a million bucks, and you have to look it. The league was very specific. Why don't you try on a couple of the shirts and maybe let Emily find you what you're looking for?"

"Hey now. I crease my jeans. What shirt? I like bright colors."

"He creases his jeans." Emily winked at him and left, presumably to find some Wranglers that Sterling would wear.

He hid his grin and went to the rack of clothing. "No... bright colors don't work on camera. You need neutrals." He pulled out something that looked pretty fancy. It was maroon and had black embroidery around the chest and shoulders. "Try this one."

Sterling wrinkled his nose but took the shirt. He stripped off his simple button-down, exposing a white long-sleeved, body-hugging shirt underneath.

Do not stare at the client.

He really didn't care if Sterling liked it. He cared that the PR pictures looked slick. One week, right? One week was all the complaining he had to listen to.

Of course, if he got to look at those abs once or twice more, that would go a long way toward making him feel better about this whole experience. Damn. That white shirt looked good against Sterling's tan skin and hugged everywhere just right.

Sterling slid the shirt on, shaking his head before he had it even on his shoulders.

He didn't ask. He didn't want to know.

Emily reached for the shoulders of the shirt to help straighten them and then tugged on the hem while Sterling was buttoning up. "That fits you well. They got the shirt measurements right." She stopped and looked at him. "What now, cowboy?"

"This all y'all need?" Sterling looked confused as hell. "No one told me I needed all new clothes."

"The league didn't tell you much, did they? You need a couple more outfits, but we have your sizes now, so Emily will just pick some things out. You also need new boots. Those are—" *Filthy.* "—worn in. That's our next stop. Go ahead and undress. I'll work out the logistics with Emily."

Jonas didn't give Sterling a chance to protest. He just escorted Emily out to the register where they talked budget, payment, and delivery details.

Sterling came back out, looking exactly the same as he'd walked in, maybe a little more grumpy.

Jonas looked at his watch. "What size are your feet, Sterling?"

"I'm a seven, but I'll shine these up, if you want."

Shiny beat-up boots were still beat-up boots.

"Emily, your boss recommended a boot place to me. Would you do me a big favor and give them a call and have a slick pair sent over to Mister Kingsolver's hotel as well? Size seven, please." He was going to tip her fifty, but for the extra help, he put a hundred-dollar bill in her hand. "I'd really appreciate it."

Emily gave him a smile. "Sure, I can handle that for you. Same credit card, right?"

"Yes. Thanks so much. Have a great night."

"Thanks. Good to meet you, Mister Kingsolver."

"Same to you, ma'am. You take care." Sterling tipped his hat to her.

Seriously, that was charming. It was nice to know that man was in there underneath all the prairie dust and growling.

He texted Louis and took Sterling outside to wait. It was fucking cold on the street. The icy wind cut right through his coat and snuck up under his cuffs. "Jesus, it's cold."

"No shit on that." Sterling put up his collar and tugged down his hat.

"I could have been on the beach right now. Warm sand in my toes, warm sun on my shoulders." *Warm body in my bed*. This was torture.

"And you got stuck with my happy ass instead. I coulda been skiing and having my momma's green chile stew. Sucks to be us."

"What is it you said? No shit on that." He laughed. "But no one's ass should be happy in this weather." Was that the car? Every damn car in Midtown was a black sedan or a yellow cab.

"I'm fairly sure no one likes this shit, but I could be wrong."

"Not in a case study of two, you're not. Oh, thank God." Louis stepped out of the car and opened the back door.

"Man, am I glad to see you."

Louis nodded. "It's a frigid day, sir. For sure."

"Cold as a witch's tit in a brass brassiere, Lord knows."

Did Sterling just say that?

"You got that right, my man!" Louis cracked up, ushering them both into the warm car and closing the door against the wind.

Oh. Warm. Jonas sighed, sticking his fingers in front of a heat vent to warm them up.

"Where to now, sir?" Louis asked, sliding into the driver's seat.

Jonas pulled out his phone. "The hotel. We've got people to meet." He checked his texts, letting everyone know they'd be at the hotel in a few minutes.

Sterling was on his phone, texting like a master, thumbs

flying. Impressive. He hadn't been sure Sterling could read, much less text like that. He was dying to find out what, or who, the cowboy was texting, though. Beer buddies? A girlfriend back home? A boyfriend back home?

Ha.

He checked his email, Instagram, read some news.... They didn't speak all the way to the hotel.

Jonas let the cowboy follow him inside and got them checked in. He'd be staying in an adjoining room, at least for tonight, and then he'd see whether Sterling could be trusted to get himself into a cab and show up to calls on time.

He had serious doubts.

He whistled as he was handed the key cards. "New wardrobe, limos, a high floor, great view, concierge service... I guess the league really does have a little cash to spend on you." He was glad about that. He could totally handle a swanky room. It didn't quite make up for the beach, but it was a start.

"I guess. I never been a world champ before."

No, really? Go figure. Jonas stopped himself from rolling his eyes. Again.

His phone buzzed, and Jonas texted Mia right back, telling her to send the manicurist to his room. He handed the cowboy a key card as they got off the elevator and squirreled the second one to Sterling's room away for himself, just in case of... well? Christ. Could be anything. "Room 2020. I'm in 2022 next door."

"Good deal. Thanks. Uh. Do you have my phone number to text and all?"

"Yeah. The league gave me your number. I need to come into your room to look it over and get the barber settled while you're in the shower. We passed him in the lobby." He didn't think he ought to leave Sterling alone for five minutes. Not until he knew the guy better. All he needed was for the cowboy to get into the minibar or something.

Those dark as night eyes went comically wide. "Uh... in my room?"

"Yeah. Haircut, manicure...?" When Sterling's expression didn't change, he got it. "Oh. Man, I really had no idea that cowboys were so modest. Would you rather I text you my number so you can call me when you're out of the shower?"

The whole modesty thing was strangely adorable. A little annoying, but adorable.

"If you don't mind, I would. I don't know you from Adam. And I ain't one of those calendar riders. I don't take my shirt off for money."

Jonas tried, he really did. He tried to hide the grin, but he totally failed. He tried really hard not to laugh too, but... calendar riders? Nope. He was pleased he managed to keep it to a short chuckle, though. "Yeah, okay, Sterling. I get it. You wouldn't want anyone to get the wrong idea."

Of course. The cowboy had to fit the stereotype, didn't he? Fucking homophobe. Jonas turned and headed for his room.

"Wrong idea about what? I just ain't used to being bare-butt nekkid with strangers. Nothing for you to get all mad about."

Usually a bathroom had a door, but it seemed like a waste of time to point that out.

"You're right. My apologies, Mister Kingsolver. Just text me when you're ready for me." Hopefully that would smooth it over. He really needed to watch himself. The WLBR was obviously big money—this assignment paid better than most—and heaven knew he needed the money. This job was a big step for him.

He and the cowboy didn't need to be friends. They didn't even need to be friendly. He was working for the league, so he just needed to make sure the guy was dressed and in the right place at the right time for one week. That was it. They had one whole week together, and then it was off to the beach.

"Yessir." The door closed and locked, and Jonas figured it was something that it hadn't slammed. Day one was not the day to blow it, right? He just really hated having to pretend. He texted so that Sterling would have his number and then let himself into his room.

4

"Lord, Chance. You know Cody and his boys are going to be here. You know it. What the hell am I s'posed to do?" Sterling sat on the edge of the tub, wishing he could have a smoke.

"He cain't take your championship, and who cares if you don't do good on the TV. You just deal with it until you can go home."

"Right. Right, I just need to buck up and stop being all titty baby." Lord have mercy, he felt like the biggest fish out of water. "Too bad they didn't send you. I could use a friend."

"All you need is confidence. You've got a great big purse and a buckle. You're a motherfucking champion, and Cody is all hat and no cattle. You've got all the friends you need."

"Right. I just got to get this done. Talk and kiss babies and sign hats." He could do that.

"Yep. Smile pretty. What is it, a week? Are you home for New Year's?"

"I sure hope so. Although everyone's going to be watching here on the TV." Which was kinda cool, really.

"Well, you let me know. I'll pick your ass up and get you some real food."

His phone buzzed as a text came in. He put Chance on speakerphone and had a look. He should have figured it'd be from Jonas.

U ready? Got a room full of stylists and food. LMK

He'd ironed his sponsor shirt that he was supposed to wear for pictures, made sure his nails were clean, and he had his good buckle on. *Ready. B over in a sec.*

K. I'll have them set up here then.

k

He wasn't sure what he'd done to make Teeth all grumpy, but he didn't think it mattered. This was going to go quick.

"You better go, huh?" Chance laughed on his end. "Someone's blowing up your phone?"

"Yeah. I got to go do this thing. I'll holler later. See you, huh?"

"Make me proud." His buddy laughed. "Later, Bit." Chance hung up, and his hotel room went quiet.

Okay. Okay. Shirt. Tuck in. Splash on some smell-good. Grab your wallet and your room key. Go.

He tapped on the door of 2022.

Jonas met him with a grin and pulled him inside. "Sterling Kingsolver, this is Dave and Annie. Dave will do your hair; Annie's got your nails."

"Pleased to meet you, Mister Kingsolver." Dave took his hand and shook it. "Come sit. How much fun is this? A bull riding champion in my chair? I found your winning ride on YouTube. It was amazing."

He was tugged into a chair and draped with a black cape.

"Uh, thank you, sir. I appreciate it." How did you get a barber in a hotel room?

"Really? You're such a brownnoser, Dave." Annie set a bowl of weird liquid on his lap and stuck his fingers in it. "He's from Maine. He doesn't know rodeo from hang gliding. And he can't ride anything for eight seconds, not even his boyfriend."

"Ah! You wound me!"

Somewhere behind him Jonas sounded like he was choking.

That was unnatural. His nails were scrubbed. Cow shit came off, after all.

He wasn't going to make a single comment about the whole boyfriend thing. It was a damn challenge, to straddle the line between what folks thought you ought to be and what you were.

Annie covered his hands with hers and gave him a sweet smile. "Relax. We've got you."

He started to smile back when Dave started wetting his hair with a misting sprayer. "So what are we going for here, Jonas?"

"Oh. Well, he's a bull rider, right? So rakish? Stylishly disheveled?"

Dave was combing through his hair like he had bugs or something. "Hm. He's got a little wave, maybe I can play with that. It's pretty short, though."

"I just got it cut last week." He liked it short on the sides and back. His folks had never been the types to allow long hair on boys, so he'd been going to Señor Martinez his entire life.

"It's a functional cut, Mister Kingsolver, but the camera loves to make a tiny glitch into a glaring flaw."

"Put some product in it," Jonas suggested, reaching over

and combing fingers through his hair without invitation. "Maybe kill the part and kind of spike it over here?"

"That could work. It would be pretty easy for you to do on your own before an interview too."

"Yeah? Give it a shot." Jonas tugged on some hair near the front and tilted his head.

Sterling tugged his head away, tossing it a little. "No pulling."

He wasn't no... life-sized doll to be dragged around.

"Hey, you guys, don't make him spill that soak." Annie came over and reset his fingers in the goop.

Jonas put a hand on his shoulder, and Dave pulled out a pair of shears. "Mister Kingsolver, just hold still, please?"

"Can't y'all call me Sterling?" Mr. Kingsolver made him feel like he was a hundred.

Dave blinked at him. "Of course. Sure. Works for me. Kingsolver is so long anyway. Although I guess Sterling is still longish. Do you use a nickname ever? Ster? Earl? Uh. Ling?" Dave laughed and started carefully trimming microscopic shards off his hair.

"No, sir." No, he'd been Little Bit his whole life, but he wasn't sharing that.

"I'm going to get started while you clip, Dave." Annie pulled his fingers out of the goo, patted them off, and replaced the bowl on his knees with a towel. "Sterling, I'm going to pull a chair up really close so I can get to your fingers. Is that going to freak you out?"

"No, ma'am. I cleaned them up real nice."

Annie gave him a smile. "I just need to clean them up a little... more. Okay?" She tucked a chair in so close in front of him they were knocking knees and set out some unpleasant-looking pokey instruments on the towel on his lap like a table. "We'll start with your cuticles."

"Are you fixin' to torture me?" he teased. "I've heard about the kinky things y'all city folk get up to."

His momma went to get her hair and nails done once a month with Granny. He knew that torture wasn't on the table, but these folks didn't know he knew.

"Why, Sterling. I'm not that kind of girl. I can't speak for Dave, though."

"Girl!"

Annie laughed. "So I'm thinking a nice hot pink... thoughts?"

"Only if you want me to get killed or it's a wear pink night."

Annie's eyes went wide. "Whoa. Is that how it is in New Mexico?"

He blinked and tilted his head, damn near impaling himself on the scissors. "Huh? Breast cancer awareness night? My momma is a survivor." He pointed to the patch on his sponsor shirt, a pink ribbon with a heart and Alba printed on it.

"I got the pink part. And good for your mom. But I meant the get killed bit." Annie winked at him.

"Oh! Oh, no. I meant at work, no?" New Mexico people tended to live and let live, mostly.

"Oh." Annie nodded.

"Cowboys," Jonas added, like that was all anyone needed to say.

"Gotcha."

The room went still until Dave broke the silence.

"Well. That was awkward. Okay, Sterling. I have to tug a little to style this—don't bark at me, please." Dave's fingers started working some gunk into his hair.

Lord have mercy. He wanted a steak as big as his head and a beer. Maybe to go out and take a walk. He'd spoken to exactly four people, and three of them didn't want him talking. He was fairly sure Louis the Driver didn't give a shit.

He needed to get something for Momma and Daddy, for Grace and Granny while he was here.

Jonas and Dave fussed with his hair, talking mostly in whispers, and Annie trimmed and filed and polished his fingernails, staying focused on her work. When they were done, Annie buffed his nails with something, and Jonas handed him a mirror. "Work for you?"

He stared at himself, wondering what they'd actually done for the last twenty minutes. It looked just about the same as always.

And he was going to wear a hat on it anyway.

"Very nice, y'all." What was he supposed to say? He looked like him. As much fuss as there'd been, he'd expected to come out looking like that big guy that played Thor in the movies—all blond and buff.

Jonas inspected his nails as Annie packed up. "Nice work, Annie."

"He should moisturize tonight. I'll leave you a bottle of cuticle cream."

"That'd be great. Thanks."

Dave took a little trimmer to the back of his neck.

"So I guess that's what they call the Sponsor Tee? I think that will be fine for the group shots, but for your interview, pick a shirt from that rack they put in your room." Jonas let his hand go. "And pick a hat too. That one you wore on the plane is pretty beat-up."

"I'll stick with my hat, thanks." That was his thing, right? The deep purple and blue band that Momma had made on her inkle loom, the beads that his sister, Grace, had added— that was his signature, that and his chaps that were purple to match.

Jonas held his eyes longer than was really comfortable and then sighed. "Fine. Annie? Dave? Let me walk you guys to the door. I really appreciate you coming out on the weekend."

"Pay's good," Annie said with a laugh.

"Good luck tomorrow."

"Thanks, Dave. We'll see. Night."

The hotel room door closed behind them.

"Hungry? I've got a tray of stuff over there, or you can order room service."

"I could eat, yeah. Thanks." So, this was harder than riding backward. At least there, you could see the shit flying toward you.

Jonas pulled the tray over and started pulling covers off things. There was a pretty good variety of stuff, considering it was hotel food. "Help yourself." The guy pulled a couple of beers out of the minifridge, opened them, and handed one to him. "They stocked me pretty well. It's not often I get beer. I could maybe get to like this cowboy celebrity thing."

"It's something else." Beer he got. "Thank you, sir."

He looked at the food and chose a half of a chicken sandwich, a bag of Cheetos.

Jonas picked up a bunch of grapes and sat on the end of the bed to eat them. "You're probably pretty beat. You feel like you're ready for this circus tomorrow?"

Not even a little. "Sure. I just need to smile and mind my manners, right?"

"That's a good start. Think about what we did in the car today so you have something to say. Don't do anything that makes you uncomfortable. Some of these guys will ask for the moon. In the end it's you in those magazines and TV ads and whatever, you know? Not them."

"What time do I need to be up and dressed?" He wasn't

at his best first thing. There was a reason they didn't ride before two at the earliest.

Jonas nodded and smiled. "Early. Sorry. We have to be there at eight for makeup and lighting, so we'll have to leave the hotel about seven thirty. I'll have hot coffee for the car ride. They'll provide breakfast. Any requests?"

"I'm easy." He didn't have to be on his all-protein diet until after the holidays, right? He could have bread and shit. "I like apple fritters."

"Oh, good call. I'll see what we can do. Oh. Mozzarella sticks." Jonas sipped his beer and then reached for the tray of food. "You've got a busy week. My advice is this should be your last beer, don't stay out late, and make sure you eat well."

"No problem. I won't show up nowhere drunk. You got a schedule or something?"

"I promised you one by morning, and you'll have it."

"Yessir." He straightened up. He was fixin' to get grumpy, and he needed to wash this shit out of his hair. "Thanks for the beer. I'll see you in the morning."

"You will." Jonas stood as well and headed for the door, not looking too disappointed that he was leaving. "Sleep well."

"You too. Night." Sterling needed to find the hotel book and read up on what all was here. There had to be a workout room, a bar, a place to sit in the lobby. Somewhere to go and chat with someone not so... shiny.

Sterling got back to his room, plugged in his phone, and sat down on the edge of the bed. Lord. He needed to get undressed, hang his shirt up, take a bath.

As soon as he closed his eyes for a second.

5

The second Sterling opened that hotel room door the next the morning, Jonas understood what he was really up against.

It wasn't the cowboy's scruffy chin; that would be fixed when they got to the shoot. It wasn't that Sterling wasn't dressed. The cowboy's midnight-dark eyes blinked sleepily at him and made even that forgivable.

"Sterling? You're... still in your pajamas."

"What do you expect? I get this friggin' email about this and that and makeup and p's and q's."

The cowboy's obvious frustration was maybe part of the problem, but it still wasn't the real issue. No, Jonas's issue was the WLBR. He was used to working for the celebrity, not for the celebrity's employer. It was like Sid had said. Sterling wasn't his client, the league was. His job was to make them happy, not this cowboy.

The beat-up look Sterling arrived with the day before worked in a "so wrong it's right" sort of way. The cowboy was easy in his skin. That was hot, and the cameras would have loved it.

But the league wouldn't.

Jonas got that the cowboy was new at this, but he still had a job to do, a paycheck to earn, and rent to pay. A job he couldn't afford to screw up.

And the cowboy was still in his damn pajamas.

Jesus, he hated being an asshole. Especially before coffee. He rubbed his forehead, wishing he'd told Sid to stuff this assignment and gone to the beach for his holiday week instead.

This was like getting coal in his stocking.

"Uh. Listen, Sterling. You need to get dressed."

"Look, I don't know what on God's green earth you want from me! I keep looking at all this fancyassed shit and—"

"Fine," he interrupted. "You want to let me into your room? I'll pick something out for you."

"Why cain't I just wear my own? I got me a good sponsor shirt. I ironed it this morning, and I know there ain't no stains."

He felt bad for this guy, he did. Sterling was obviously not used to being in anyone's spotlight. "Yeah. Thing is, Sterling, you're representing the league now, and you have to look the part. I'll just grab you a few things. Can you let me in, please?"

"Sure. Come on in." Sterling stepped back and let him by. "Cain't believe this place don't have a coffee maker."

"I can get you one. It might just be a little Keurig, but it'll be something." He didn't look around or get nosy. He just went right to the untouched rack of clothing in the corner of Sterling's hotel room, unzipped the cover, and opened it up.

He pulled out a pair of jeans, the Western shirt with the fancy embroidery on it, and a brand-new belt. Sterling watched him without a word, eyes like stone, then held a hand out for the clothes.

"I'll just wait in the hall? Pull those boots on too, please."
God, he felt like a dick.

"Yessir." There wasn't any anger, though, as Sterling
carefully pulled off his T-shirt and laid it out on the bed, but
there wasn't an ounce of give in the tone either.

God, look at that—Sterling was tanned and muscled, a
single, wild scar like a lightning bolt from shoulder to waist.
Jonas was suddenly very aware of two things. One, Sterling
might be pint-sized, but looking at that build, there was no
question the cowboy could kick his ass. And two, Jonas
really liked looking at that build.

He swallowed, noting that not only was he totally
staring, but his mouth had gone dry. He needed to leave the
room.

"I'm gonna... uh. You're not a calendar rider, remember?"
Jonas backed up a couple of steps. "Yeah. I'll be... outside."
He hurried out into the hall.

Jesus. He and Grindr needed a date tonight.

It took Sterling only a minute to open the door—jeans
on, one boot on, one boot off. "I need your laundry bag."

"My...?" *Shut up, dickhead, and get the man what he needs.*
"Hang on." What the hell did Sterling need his laundry bag
for? He ducked into his room, grabbed it, and then hurried
back out into the hall. "Here."

"Thank you." Sterling took the boot, leaned against the
doorframe, and stuck his foot in the bag. Then he pulled the
new boot on and tore the bag away.

He sighed. There was no way he was going to apologize
for doing his damn job. This was going to be a long fucking
week. And it was starting with them being late. "You almost
ready?"

"Yep." Sterling grabbed the shirt and his hat, then

headed out, buttoning as he walked. On the way down in the elevator, Sterling unfastened his jeans and tucked in.

"There's a Starbucks in the lobby. I ordered on my phone so we can just grab it on our way out. Oh, and the girl I talked to said they'll have fritters for you. If you have a lunch request let me know. I'll arrange it. And I emailed you the schedule for the rest of the week like you asked." He just wanted his coffee, a bagel, and to get this day over with.

"Thank you, sir." Sterling looked stiff, uncomfortable, but the man could move.

The car ride was quiet, each of them sipping their coffee and lost somewhere in thought. When they arrived for the shoot, they were ushered into the building, shuttled through a locked door, and whisked off to a private elevator. He started to feel a little better. He might not know anything about bull riding, but this was one gig he knew well. The media life of a celebrity—photographers, makeup artists, PAs, reporters... this was his kind of circus.

"We'll get Mister Kingsolver straight to makeup, and you can have a look at the interview questions." The darling little PA smiled at him. "We'll do that first and then the shoot, then lunch, then the other cowboys show up."

"Got it." He squinted over at Sterling, thinking over his instructions for the PA. "Um, go easy on the hair product, give him a shave, and nobody touches his hat. Okay?"

"Of course. Mister Kingsolver, if you'll come with me?"

Sterling gave him a panicked look, but the PA got a charming smile. "Yes, ma'am."

"Cowboy up!" He grinned at Sterling. "I'm gonna grab those interview questions and find your breakfast." With a smile like that, Sterling was going to do just fine in the dressing room.

He wandered through the set for the interview and

pitched a little fit until they switched out the background that showed off all the other cowboys for one with just the WLBR logo and sponsors. They wanted to look at cowboys, they could look at his cowboy. Sterling was the champion, right?

The stage manager came by with a clipboard and the list of questions, and he looked them over but decided a couple of the personal ones were going to be up to Sterling, so he stuck them under his arm, grabbed a couple of fritters and two coffees, and headed for makeup. Hopefully he hadn't left Sterling to his own devices too long.

Sterling sat in the chair, hat in his hands, perfectly still. Makeup had cleaned him up, eradicated the circles under his eyes, smoothed out his skin tone. The dark eyes were like marbles, hard and shiny in the lights. God, he could see the tension, could feel it pour off the man.

He could only feel so bad for Sterling, though. The first one would be the hardest, and by the end of the week it would be easier. Or at least he hoped so, because he'd heard Sterling was headed off on a much longer publicity tour after this. It was a big pill to swallow.

"One apple fritter and a large, hot coffee." He tilted his head at Sterling. "Can I hang your hat up for you so you can eat?"

Sterling glanced down at his hat, like he'd forgotten he had it. "Sure. Are they done messing with me?"

He set Sterling's food down on the vanity and hung up the man's hat on a rack right next to the mirror. "Yes, I think so. You look a little.... Are you okay? Nervous?"

"Sure. I ain't never done this before." Sterling stood and began pacing, slow and steady.

He watched, letting Sterling breathe a minute. "I've got the questions. You want to see them? I think the hardest one is...." He looked at the paper and read the question. "What does it feel like to be the dark horse and displace the favorite?"

"It felt fucking wonderful." Sterling's lip curled, the expression suddenly lit up and fiery. "It was the highlight of my season."

"I bet." *Wow.* That was a good look. He found himself studying it a bit before he remembered he had a couple of other questions to ask about. "That's a great answer. Just leave out the curse words."

He looked over the list again. "They want to know what you're going to do with the money. I'd say that's exploitive. I wouldn't answer that one. You didn't win the fucking lottery. You earned that money."

"Fair enough. My bank account ain't nobody's business but mine."

Oh, he almost felt sorry for the interviewer. "Most of these are what we talked about yesterday—why you ride, what's your background, what do you like to do when you're not riding. They have a few questions about your family. Just remember not to say anything you wouldn't put out on the internet."

"I won't." Sterling walked, the pace steady and sure, the click of Sterling's boots maddening.

"Sterling. Sit. Eat something. You're going to be fine. You want a laugh? I made them take down a background that had all these other rodeo cowboys on it and put one up with just the logo." He gave Sterling a toothy grin. "Those guys can wait their turn."

"Yeah? That's good. Thanks." Sterling took a deep breath. "I can't eat. They put stuff all over my face."

"You can eat. I brought you a fork and knife. And they'll touch you up right before."

"All right, Mister Kingsolver, we're ready for you." The little PA was back, and he instantly regretted not asking her name.

"Yes, ma'am. Just let me get my hat." Sterling seemed to grow stiff and starched.

He put a hand on Sterling's shoulder as the cowboy passed by. "You've got this," he said quietly. "All this pomp and circumstance is smoke and mirrors. You're the real deal."

It was cheerleading, sure. It was like talking up a boxer before a fight. But he meant it too. "I'll be in the dark behind the cameraman. You won't be able to see me, but I'll be there."

"Thanks." Sterling lifted his chin. "Let's do this."

6

S terling stood in the shadows, pretending he was on his phone. The only reason he wasn't running away was the new boots had rubbed him raw and every fucking step made his feet scream.

Cody Ball was here with Travis McMartin and Cooter Parrish, the other Americans in the top ten. They were like sharks, like vicious, toothy asshats that could smell blood.

And good Lord, wasn't there blood in the water?

Mr. Teeth had stopped smiling after the "interview" and hadn't even spoken to him during the lunch break. He hadn't bothered to eat. He'd figure something else at the hotel.

Sterling wasn't totally sure what he'd done wrong, but he knew he had felt like a poser—itchy shirt, jeans that didn't feel like his, shit on his face and his hair. He didn't want to be someone else; he liked being him. He'd been good enough to ride the bulls, dammit.

All he had to do was survive this.

Jonas headed for him, wearing a frown and making a

"wrap it up" gesture with one hand. "They want to get started with the shoot in a second."

There was laughter from Cody's crew, and Jonas looked over, watching them and waiting for him to get off the phone.

Like he was really on it. *Okay, Bit. Do this.*

He put his phone in his pocket and offered Mr. Teeth a smile. "Ready."

He started to take a step forward, but his handler got in the way, physically stopping him with a hand on his chest. Green eyes met his, and he'd swear there was more in them than pissed off. They actually seemed sincere.

"Listen, Sterling. I know you'd rather be anywhere but here right now. Frankly, I feel the same way. Just shake off the interview and do your job, okay? These... *gentlemen* seem like they know the drill. Just focus. Smile for the camera, keep your mouth shut, and I promise I'll get you out of here the minute you're done."

Huh. So "gentlemen" apparently also meant "asshole" out in Yankeeland. Good to know.

"Fair enough." He nodded once and tipped his hat, and then he headed over. Mouth shut. Smile. Then he could go. He could totally do this.

"Hey, Little Bit. You enjoying your one good year?" Cody's voice was dripping with venom, and Sterling fought not to respond.

He got it. Sterling understood more than anyone knew. The bullfighters would be told that he was toxic, and he'd take the hits. The judges would call him for penalties in the chute, slaps. There would be someone in the parking lot, someone in the locker room, someone that was going to come after him, and someday he'd lose out. He got it.

It didn't matter. He was a cowboy, not an athlete.

He had a code; he had to face his folks. Hell, he had to face Grace.

"Mister Ball." Jonas gave Cody a nod. "I'm Jonas Burke. I've heard a lot about you."

"Burke." Cody nodded back. "You representing the little cowboy that could?"

"I'm employed by the league, actually. Ready to get to work?"

"Absolutely. I have the million-dollar smile, with or without the championship. Do you have all your teeth in, Bit?"

No talking. None. Zero.

"The photographer prefers to work quietly, Mister Ball."

McMartin and Parrish both broke into barely controlled giggles.

"Did he just tell you to shut up?" Parrish pretended to whisper to Cody.

Jonas gave Sterling's chest a thump and got out of the way while the photographers did their thing, posing them and snapping pictures.

One of the assistant guys—a kid about his height and thin as a rail—came up to touch up their makeup, and Cody started in. "I bet Bit wears this shit when he's home. Tell me, buddy"—Cody poked the assistant in the center of the chest, hard—"you ever seen this asshole on your Grindr shit?"

Quiet. No talking. Mouth shut. Don't hit the motherfucker. What tickled the fuck out of him and kept him from popping Cody in the mouth was the irony—Ball didn't have the foggiest clue he was gay. Stupid shit.

Jonas was on the move, though, and whisked the kid away without a word.

The photographer's assistant, a tall woman with thick

dark hair, posed them all this way and that, making him stand much closer to Cody than he cared to.

Cody kept making his comments, but they stopped eventually when he wasn't getting the reaction he wanted from anyone but McMartin and Parrish, who even he had to know would have kissed his bare ass if he wanted them to.

Sterling stood, focusing on keeping his smile on, keeping his eyes open, and keeping his fist out of Cody's face.

"All right, that looks good, guys. We're done. I'll get your reps a link when I get them online." The photography crew started packing up equipment.

"Can we catch a ride with y'all? They have us in the same hotel."

Jesus fuck, could these guys be any more pissed? He'd rode a bull, sure, but they'd been the ones that had fallen off.

"Sure. I'll just switch the sedan to a limo." Jonas appeared from the darkness behind the cameras, texting. "The league would probably appreciate it if I got you guys back to the hotel in one piece anyway. Can we be civil on the ride, please?"

Parrish rolled his eyes. "Think you can keep your hands to yourself for the drive, Bit?"

He arched one eyebrow, looked Parrish up and down slowly, then let his lip curl. "Not a problem."

"Come on, Sterling, let's get you cleaned up." Jonas herded him off set and back to makeup, where the friendly girl from earlier was waiting for them.

"All done for the day, guys?"

Jonas nodded. "Yeah, he just needs to get the makeup off."

The rest of the cowboys joined them a second later,

taking up chairs along the wall of mirrors. He took note of where Jonas placed himself, between him and Parrish, and blocking his view of all of them.

He closed his eyes, praying for a Coke machine somewhere along the way. He was so fucking thirsty, and his head hurt.

Surely if he couldn't see them, they couldn't see him.

"Are you taking that makeup off, Little Bit, or touching it up before you go out on the town tonight?" McMartin got a good laugh from the other guys.

Someone had to have said something. He hadn't done much, but sometimes a guy had to have a little touch. Or hell, maybe they were just trying to needle him.

Jesus, was he doing something wrong by not acting pissed?

"Breathe," Jonas said quietly. "We'll be rid of these guys soon."

He nodded and met Jonas's eyes in the mirror. He was so fixin' to get grumpy.

Jonas looked back at him. "You need anything for the ride? You want a snack or something? You barely ate."

"A Coke. I'd kill for a Dr Pepper, please." Damn, he was growly sounding, and he didn't even mean to be, but he wanted these clothes and boots off.

"No need to kill." He got a flash of those teeth.

The makeup folks were done with them pretty quick. The limo that pulled up was all black with dark windows and looked like the Secret Service or Elvis or someone ought to be inside. Instead it was him and a bunch of assholes, sitting their Wranglers on smooth leather seats and playing with the stereo.

He didn't play. He didn't text. He sat there and waited. All he had to do was get to the hotel, and eventually he did. Without anyone throwing a punch. Miracle of miracles.

They streamed into the lobby in a pack, but Jonas waved him on toward the elevators and ushered the rest of them to the reception desk so they could get checked in.

"I'm going to grab you a soda, okay? I'll bring it over. Maybe a sandwich too."

"That would be good." He didn't have any smiles left. "Thanks."

With the way his feet hurt, it seemed like he'd just barely made it to his room and parked his ass in a chair when Jonas came knocking. Of course, he'd also closed his eyes for a minute, so maybe it had been longer than it seemed.

"Just come in." He wasn't moving another step in these boots.

"I brought you a six-pack of Dr Pepper, a sandwich, and they're bringing you a coffee maker in a little while." Jonas set everything down on a table by the window. "Whoa. You look tired."

"Yeah. Little." He pulled one boot off and heard Jonas gasp. *Oh, fuck. Don't get all offended about my stocking feet.* He looked up to snarl, when he saw the utter shock in Jonas's face, Jonas's eyes on his foot. He looked down—his sock was drenched in blood and lymph.

Oops.

"Thought they were blistering."

"Jesus, Sterling." Jonas got him a towel from the bathroom and spread it out on the floor. "Get the other one off. I'm going to run get some ice."

By the time he opened his mouth to say that Jonas didn't have to bother, the man was gone. So he took his other boot off and pondered how bad it was going to suck to rip off his socks.

Jonas came back with two buckets of ice and set them down on the floor by his feet. "Wet washcloths maybe," Jonas suggested, already on the way back to the bathroom. "How bad do they hurt?"

"Worse than a bee sting, less than getting trampled."

"That's kind of a wide range, cowboy." Jonas dropped right to the floor by his feet and looked up at him, a little hint of a smile and a flash in those green eyes. "Bigger than a bread box?"

"Smaller than a whale." He'd loved that game when he was a little boy. "Lord, what a day."

What pretty eyes. The thought was sudden and sure, and he was tickled shitless that Jonas couldn't hear it.

"It was a long one. You want me to help you get these socks off? Oh. I brought...." Jonas sat up on his knees and dug through his pockets, then handed him a bottle of Tylenol and a box of Band-Aids with a laugh. "That's my entire first aid kit."

"You are doing better than me, man." He accepted the Tylenol and took three. "Okay, I need to just get these socks off before they stick."

"Yeah." Jonas reached for the cuff of one sock and started to peel it off, easing the fabric over the spots that were already stuck to the blisters. "Why didn't you say anything?"

"What were we going to do?" Let the guys rag him? Bah. He was just glad to get the itchy shirt off.

"Well, we could have maybe wrapped your feet or something? I don't know, but this looks so painful." Jonas managed to get both socks off for him without much more than making him wince a little.

"Damn, that's impressive." He was going to have to find a

shit-ton of moleskin. Most of the blisters had busted, and tomorrow they were going to hurt like nothing going.

"I wish I had Neosporin and, like, New-Skin or something. I'll run out for you after we get this cleaned up. God. Burn those fucking boots." The damp washcloth cooled his skin as Jonas dabbed at the blisters, cleaning up the blood.

Then Jonas wrapped ice inside a wet cloth and pressed it to the bottom of his foot. He arched, a deep moan slipping right out of him.

"Whoa." A heavy hand landed on his thigh, holding his leg still, and the ice stayed in place. "Easy."

"S-sorry." He blinked, his body responding totally inappropriately to the adrenaline and the rush and the feel of that hand on his leg.

"Just want to... uh." Jonas cleared his throat, eyes glued to him from where the man knelt on the floor. "Get the, uh, get the swelling down."

"Yeah." Lord, his tongue was all big in his mouth, his cock filling in his jeans.

Jonas lifted his hand away suddenly and looked at it like he'd burned it or something. After another second he stood up. "So. I'm going to get a couple more towels for you. You need to ice these feet for a bit."

"Thanks." *Dammit.* "You don't have to, really."

He didn't think Jonas would get his panties in a wad, but he didn't need any slips.

Jonas came back with a couple more damp towels. "I apologize if I made you uncomfortable."

"No worries. I'm fine." *Yeah, uncomfortable in my jeans.* Christ on a sparkly purple crutch.

"You want to put your feet up? It might be a good idea. I

could pack them up in some ice for you." Jonas offered him a hand up. "Get comfy on the bed, maybe?"

He stood and hissed. Oh, that was like dipping his feet in fire. He danced on the way over to the bed, feeling like an idiot, but he was walking on knives.

Jonas helped, letting him lean and getting him turned around so he could sit. "God. That's it. You wear your own boots from now on. If the photographers don't like it, they can leave your feet out." Jonas got him settled, then sat on the edge of the bed and with careful fingers started gently wrapping and packing his feet in ice.

"They're nice boots. You got to just wear them in a little at a time, right?" It was a rare set that didn't bring up one or two blisters, after all.

"I guess, but all day? Your feet might take all week to recover." Jonas finished up and then started wandering around his room. The TV remote landed on the bed beside him. Jonas set the sandwiches and a couple of Dr Peppers there too, and his phone on the bedside table.

"I'm going to let you get some rest. Tomorrow is the hospital visit in the afternoon, but you have the morning off. Sleep in."

"I can so do that." Wow. Jonas was crazy organized. Sterling barely managed to get all his shit in his go-bag. Impressive.

Jonas looked around the room, like the guy was making sure nothing was out of place or about to set him on fire or something, then headed out the door. "Just text me if you need anything."

The door closed quietly behind Jonas, and his hotel room went still.

God. God, he just wanted to go home and enjoy his one big success.

He closed his eyes, but all he could see were pretty green eyes. That sure wasn't going to help him sleep. This publicity shit was hard enough already without that awkward distraction too.

Sterling didn't know how people did it. He wasn't shy—he went out for handshakes and signatures after every event, and he met with his sponsors. He'd even done ads for Jackson Motors and Pecina's Cafe. This all-day shit in strange shirts was something else. Not only that, but with Pecina's came tacos.

He picked up the remote, put some movie on the TV, and reached for his phone, which buzzed the second he put his hand on it.

Hey, Bit! Kiss any babies today? Did you put that dickhead Ball in his place? Chase. Thank God.

Didn't kiss anyone. Didn't kill anyone either. Yay *g*

Damn. Does that make it a good day or a bad one? LOL

Long. Just long. Sitting here with my feet in ice.

That sucks. We're waiting for the pics to hit the internet to see your million dollar smile not your blistered heels man.

Yeah yeah. U hear that Ball was owed that championship? He grinned at the sarcasm, because the other option was to cry, and that just wasn't going to happen.

Masterson wanted you to throw it, right? I figured it was cuz of Ball. Plus he looked like he was gonna cry when your 8 secs were up.

Not an athlete right? He was more than a guy that had a good free arm and balance.

Hell no. So they promised him? Assholes. I'm glad you stayed on. Is Ball pissed? You worried?

Yes. Yes. A little. His phone rang in his hands, and he damn near dropped it. "What?"

"Don't you let them make you quit, Bit."

"Stop it, Chance. I ain't. I just... you know they're going to murder my ass. I'm going to get trampled." He could do it without buddies, but without bullfighters? Shit.

"You got friends. We got your back, huh? Maybe Ball will flame out before next season."

"Maybe. I could push him under a bus."

Chance hooted like a big ole barn owl. "I like it! Trip him in front of one of those underground trains, right? Works in the movies!"

"Yeah. Tomorrow I'm going to go see kids at the hospital." He was looking forward to that. Him and kids got along like a house afire.

"Ah. The charity poster." Chance laughed. "Can you imagine Cody with those kids? 'Be like me! Get a personal trainer and eat your vegetables!' They'll be way more impressed with the real deal."

"Yeah. And you know me. I've got this." He peeked at his feet.

"You do, Bit. Mira, look. That poser gets in your face this week, you just show him how a cowboy handles assholes."

"Yeah. I'm at the end of my rope, buddy. I mean, dangling." He started to laugh, the thought of swinging on a rope like a kung-fu guy and kicking Cody Ball right in the face.

"Hang him with it." Chance didn't really sound like he was joking.

"You got my back, huh?" Not that he was scared, but....

"You know it. You need bail? You need me on a plane? You need me to bury a body, I'm there, Bit."

"Fair enough." He sat up and said his goodbyes, then snarfed down the sandwich, which wasn't anywhere near enough.

Maybe he would just put on his own boots, head downstairs, and find some french fries, a beer.

THE HOTEL BAR WAS BUSY, packed full of slick-looking folks in suits and heels, and even if that was his crowd, he might faint waiting on his fries.

Okay, there had to be a bar or a diner or a coffee shop right here, didn't there? This was a busy city, open twenty-four hours, and it wasn't late.

Out on the sidewalk, he pulled his hat down and his collar up against the chilly wind and hoped to find something not too far off because the frozen drizzle felt like tiny little needles blowing in his face. About two blocks down, he saw neon, which no matter what it said was the universal sign for jukeboxes and beer.

Those were two things he approved of, God help him.

He paid his cover and slipped in, the scent of peanuts and beer like heaven. Oh, he had only been legal a year and a half or so, but he knew honkytonks. He knew this.

The place was bigger than it looked from the outside, the bar stretching back quite a way down one wall. Square tables lined the other, and the area in between was either a passageway or a dance floor depending on where you were standing.

He got to the bar and got his draft, then turned to find three cowboys surrounding him.

Fuck-a-doodle-goddamn-doo.

He tightened his fingers around his bottle. "Evening, gentlemen."

"It is that." Cody reached out and took the bottle out of his fingers. "Are you even legal, Little Brat?"

"Bit. It's Bit, Cody," McMartin said, grinning.

"Is it? Well, it's a good thing I don't give a fuck, then." Cody leaned in close. "I'm going to castrate your queer ass, Little Fuck, and then I'm going to make sure you never ride again."

"You might try." That was all the monologuing he was fixin' to do. He drew back and let fly. They didn't call him a cowboy for nothin'.

7

I t took Jonas two blocks, the two city block walk from the hotel to the fucking bar, to realize that no amount of breathing and telling himself to be cool was going to work.

It was barely midnight. It had only taken Kingsolver two fucking hours to find trouble. Two hours to eat a sandwich, leave the hotel, and get into a fight bad enough they had to close the goddamn bar. Two hours before someone from the league woke him up with a phone call and read him the riot act.

The light of day was going to be ugly.

He stared at the entrance to the bar, trying to decide what he was going to say, and finally decided he'd better not open his stupid mouth at all. Nobody was going to like what came out of it.

"Bar's closed, sir." A cop looked him in the eye.

"Yeah. I'm here to pick up Sterling Kingsolver." He handed the cop a business card, and the guy let him inside.

Sterling stood there, shirt torn up, lip split, one wrist bandaged. His hat was a little worse for wear, but the man was standing.

He couldn't say the same for Cody Ball.

Shut your mouth, Burke. Shut your goddamn mouth. Keep your mouth shut.

He caught Sterling's eyes and gave the cowboy a long, hard stare. Then he angled his head toward the door. "Let's go."

Sterling nodded once, then leaned away from the bar. The motion was quite possibly the hottest thing he'd ever seen—pure will, heat, and cowboy wrapped in a little package.

Bad enough he was pissed off, but now he was pissed off and half-hard too. Jesus Fucking Christ.

Jonas stepped aside and let Sterling go out the door first, following the cowboy into the icy rain. The cold air actually felt good, woke him up a little, cleared his head, but he doubted it was going to do much to really cool either of them off.

Sterling walked beside him, water dripping off his hat. "I guess the league called you?"

"Yeah. They called me." They'd called. Sid had called. The cops had fucking called.

He noted that Sterling had not called.

"So, what? I beat up the bastard and y'all get all snippy? He deserved it. I ain't apologizing."

"No?" Oh, steam built up fast behind the lid he'd been keeping on his temper, and he stopped dead in the middle of the wet sidewalk. "Not apologizing?"

"No, sir. He wants to kill me, he'd better learn that he has to work for it." Sterling stared at him, chin set.

God-fucking-dammit. Something in that stare made his balls ache.

"Oh, I see. Make him work for it. Well, you sure showed him, didn't you? You're feeling pretty proud of yourself?"

"What the hell is your—"

"You know what? I was supposed to be in sunny Curaçao getting my tan on this week, you smug little asshole. But instead I'm still here, still in New York in the freezing cold. Why? Because some pompous cowboy bull rider league hired me to spend my holiday week holding your hand, playing fucking cheerleader, and making sure you toe the line and smile for the camera without getting into trouble."

So much for keeping his mouth shut. Well, he was on a roll now.

"And you know what else? I've been working my ass off for more than just the paycheck. I mean, I need that too, but this is a solid step up for me. A big one. But you've been nothing but... ugh! I am not going to sit quietly by while your fucking league reams me a new one over your million-dollar redneck cowboy ass. How dare you make me look like I can't do my fucking job? Screw you, man! You and your fucking homophobic rodeo clown buddies can kiss my pale, queer ass. You wanna fight someone? Step right up, Tiny. You don't grow up in Jersey City and not know how to throw a goddamn punch. Bring it on."

"Feel better?"

His fingers twitched, and he stared back, so ready to throw that punch, but he decided this wasn't a game he felt like playing. "Go to hell." He turned and headed into the hotel again. Jesus. What was he doing? He was going to get his own ass fired this time.

"People been telling me that for a while now." Sterling followed along, totally unfazed by his outburst. The son of a bitch didn't even seem drunk.

"Yeah? Maybe it's time you listened." *He's a paycheck, idiot. He might be a hot paycheck, but he's still a paycheck. Don't blow this.*

"Maybe so."

He kept going, making it about halfway to the elevator before he realized the bootheels weren't clicking along behind him anymore.

What the hell now? He turned around to see what the cowboy was up to.

Sterling was at the little gift shop, pulling two Dr Peppers out of the cooler before choosing a Snickers.

He sighed and waited. Sterling was going back to the hotel room, and then he would camp out in the hall if he had to in order to keep the cowboy in there.

Five days. He had to watch this guy for five more days, and then he could get a tan while Sid was cooking up his next big assignment.

Sterling glanced at him. "I ain't running away. You want a Coke? I got two."

"No." He resisted the urge to point out that it was a Dr Pepper. He hit the Up button and stepped back. "Thank you."

Sterling opened one of the bottles and drank deep, throat working. Then they stepped into the elevator and the doors closed. "I didn't even get my beer, much less my french fries before they started in."

He was wet, he was cold, and he really didn't feel like a vendetta between a bull riding champion and a sad, mad, cowboy reject was his bailiwick. Actually, come morning, Sterling might not be his problem anymore either. Sid sounded about ready to fire him. He was going to have to do some fast talking if he wanted to keep working for deep pockets. "I'll make a call when we get back and get you a bodyguard."

"I don't need a bodyguard. I wanted a fucking order of

french fries. I was hungry." Sterling stepped out of the elevator. "I'll meet you downstairs at eleven."

"Might be me, might be someone else from my agency. They'll find you. Next time, when your handler says call if you need anything? Call. You'll get fries without the side of fractured fist."

"Right. Mira, look. No one said I wasn't allowed to leave. I didn't get drunk. I didn't start the fight. I did finish it. Sue me. We have to survive four more fucking days. I will do the hospital, and then I'll call them at the home office and tell them no one wants to talk to me no more."

"You've got this all figured out, don't you? Good. I hope it works out for you and you can go home and enjoy your million-fucking-dollar purse. I need to get to bed. I have a call with my boss early in the morning, during which I'm expecting to be fired. Good night."

Hopefully this would be the last time he had to talk with Mr. No Apologies.

"Was I just supposed to let them wale on me?" The words were soft. "I'll call Masterson tomorrow and tell him I snuck out and you didn't know. Night."

Sterling's door closed with a click.

Shit. He marched over to the closed door and raised his hand to knock but stopped himself at the last minute and braced his hand against it instead. "Dammit."

Sterling shouldn't have left the room. The guy was tired and his feet were beat to hell—why would he go out?

Jonas didn't need to care. There was no reason in the world why he should. It was a one-week gig, that was all. He never would have crossed paths with the cowboy if not for this fluke job, and come the end of the week, he'd have no reason to ever again.

He did seem to care, though. He just... did. But he couldn't knock. He pushed off the door and headed back to his room.

8

Sterling had been up at six and spent the last four hours drinking coffee and playing on his phone. God, he wasn't going to have to worry about dieting. This whole big-city thing was hard on a man's stomach.

He dialed Masterson's number as soon as it turned nine in Dallas.

"Did you have to break his nose, asshole?"

"I think if you ask around, that was the bartender. She was amazing. I just got him on the ground. She kicked him in the face."

"I'm going to have him press charges."

"If you could do that, you'd have had me in the police station, and you don't. I just want to get this done. I won the season, whether or not you like it, like I told you. Back off."

The laugh was low and nasty as hell. "What do you want, Kingsolver?"

"To let you know that the PR guy didn't know I'd left. I didn't know I was on house arrest. I do now."

"Do you?" Masterson snorted. "Bet that chaps your ass."

"Yep."

"Good. You remember that. You don't go nowhere without him, get it?" He heard the pure glee in Masterson's voice. "Both your jobs depend on it."

Jonas would be so pleased.

Still. Jonas still had a job, and what did he care? He could handle four more days of this.

"Did you hear me, boy? You've fucked up enough, and now we're stuck with you."

"Uh-huh. I hear you. Talk at you later, man." He hung up and got dressed. He'd washed the sizing out of the shirts in the sink last night and had ironed one dry. He'd reshaped his hat even.

He was ready to face the day. Maybe he could grab another candy bar downstairs.

But getting downstairs early bit him in the ass. His handler was sitting on a couch in the middle of the lobby, where nobody coming or going could get by unnoticed. Not that Sterling was hard to spot anyway—he was the black sheep in the cowboy hat.

Jonas stood up as soon as their eyes met. Looked like the guy hadn't gotten any sleep either.

Okay, so he could wait for the sugar rush.

"Mornin'." He tipped his hat, then stood there and waited for whatever the guy needed to yell about. The shirt was pressed and good, the jeans were theirs, and Jonas had said to wear his own boots today.

Jonas nodded, looking him over, and then smiled at him. No flash of teeth, just a smile, and something in those eyes made the green look darker than usual. "Come on." Jonas walked past him, leading him out the door and onto the sidewalk.

One day, he promised himself. *One day you can come here and see stuff and just gawk.* He'd bet Grace would love to see pictures of all the lights and things. He'd have to get her postcards.

It was still chilly this morning, but the sun was out and so were lots of people. Jonas was walking at a good clip at first, black jeans and black coat blending in with the suits and overcoats headed in the opposite direction on the sidewalk. The guy glanced over his shoulder after about half a block and slowed down so they were walking together, but still didn't seem to have anything to say.

They walked another block or so before Jonas stopped and pulled open a door. It wasn't a hospital; it was a restaurant. "After you."

He wanted to ask, but he was going with *keep your mouth shut, stupid*, so he just went in.

Once they were seated, Jonas ordered them each a coffee and opened the menu. "We've got two hours, and I hate to face the day hungry."

Oh, thank God. He was starving. "I hear that."

Lord, this was awkward as all get-out.

"How do your feet feel today?" Jonas reached for a mug of coffee, and the unmistakable scent of Old Spice drifted across the table.

Oh, that was fine as frog hair. "Tender as hell, but the ice helped."

"And your hand? Your lip doesn't look too bad."

"If it's broke, it's a hairline. Fingers all work." He chuckled and wiggled as best he could.

"Good, because the kids are going to want to shake it." Jonas gave him a wink. "I had some things delivered for you to give out—little cowboy hats, cowboy coloring books, a whole rainbow of bandanas."

"Good deal. Thank you." The babies loved stuff like that. "How long do we get to stay?"

He was ready for some joy.

"You're scheduled for two hours, but no one is going to throw you out if you're doing some good." Jonas sipped coffee and put the menu down, and a waitress was over in seconds. "Have whatever you want. It's on the league." Jonas's tone was as dry as the Sahara.

"Two eggs over easy, crispy bacon, toast, and whatever fruit deal y'all have." That was easy. They wouldn't have chile here.

Jonas looked at him and then at the waitress. "I'll have exactly the same thing, please. And more coffee when you get a chance? Thanks." She took their menus and disappeared, and the table got quiet.

He wasn't sure whether to tell Jonas that he'd called Masterson or not. Obviously the man wasn't fired, so maybe not....

Jonas tapped a finger on the table. "So... the answer is no." Green eyes finally met his. "I couldn't expect you to just let them wale on you."

"Yeah. That would have sucked." He shot Jonas part of a grin, more than willing to make up. "It sucks that they woke you up."

"No, what sucks is that you didn't call me, but I get it. You're not used to this celebrity thing. There are rules, and my boss gave me an earful this morning about how I should have made them much clearer. But as you can probably tell, I wasn't fired."

Celebrity? Him? Shee-it. "Thank God for that."

He hadn't known he couldn't leave the hotel. Hell, it hadn't even occurred to him.

"So, as things stand, if you had to go out and get in a fight last night, I'm really fucking glad you flattened that asshole. I was about ready to feed him his own scrotum after what he did to that makeup artist."

He nodded once. "That was bullshit. I was fixin' to get in the middle of it, but you did good. I don't hold with that nonsense."

"Good to hear. Thanks. Our new rules are that I'm not supposed to let you out of my sight." Jonas shrugged. "So I figured if we were going to be spending every waking moment together, I wanted to clear the air. Are we good?"

"Yes, sir." He wasn't sure what all he'd done, but whatever. He had coffee. Eggs were coming. He was okay.

"Great." Jonas smiled at him. "Oh, did they tell you they're done with you on Thursday now? Seems Cody got his face busted by a bartender, and now he can't do photographs."

"No. That's good. You'll be off for New Year's Eve, then." He bet flying home on the thirty-first would be neat, with all the fireworks.

"I'll be on a plane to a warmer climate. I might even leave Friday night if I can get you a flight." Plates landed in front of them, along with a big pile of bacon to share. "Oh yeah. That's what I'm talking about."

"Don't worry about me. You're off work Thursday, huh? You can get your champagne on the plane Friday." He grabbed the salt and pepper for his eggs.

"I have to worry about you, remember? I'm not off until they tell me I'm off, so we'll see." Jonas was already eating, munching on a piece of bacon. "Do you know how long you're home before the national tour starts? Do you have a few days, or do they send you right back out?"

"The first event is the last week of January." He'd be spending some of the break with Grace. Momma and Daddy wanted to go on a vacation for a week or so.

"So you roll right back into it, huh? Crazy. You'll barely get a break." Jonas shrugged and laughed, and he noted that those rows of white teeth were less visible when the smiles were more genuine. "Of course I'm only getting a week, so I guess you're doing okay. I won't meet up with my friends. They're all down there this week, but I still want the sun. I'll meet some people. I usually do. Do you have a lot of friends at these events?"

"I used to. I bet I have a lot less now." He dipped his toast in his yolk. "My best buddy is Chance. Chance Leonards. He's a good man. He was a team roper, but he's working the big show now."

Chance's guy, Bobby, had got hurt a couple years ago and decided to start working their ranch.

"Less... because you beat out an arrogant asshole? How many friends can he have?"

"Lots." Because Sterling hadn't played the game, because he hadn't done what they wanted—he was never going to win an event again. It was how it worked. You either followed your heart or the rules. "But I'll know who my real friends are."

"I guess you will. Not a bad thing." Jonas drained the last of his coffee. "We should get moving. Have you had enough?" He called the waitress over and got the check.

"Sure." He wanted to take the rest of the bacon with him. He did snatch another piece and ate it quick.

Jonas pulled out his phone, texted something, and then got up. "Car is down the block."

The sidewalk was much less busy now than it was earlier, and they could easily walk side by side down the block to the car. Jonas seemed pretty relaxed, a big change even from earlier that morning. "This is much better weather than last night." Jonas opened the car door for him.

It wasn't a fancy car, just an ordinary Uber, and the back seat was a little tight.

"Does it snow here sometimes?" It snowed like crazy up where he was from.

"Yeah. Actually we're expecting some Thursday. Not a lot, just six inches or so, but enough to make things pretty. I was hoping all that cold rain would turn to snow last night, but no luck."

Oh, that would be cool. He did love the snow. He had a great pair of cross-country skis. Maybe he'd go for a wander when he got home.

His thigh was warm where Jonas's rubbed against him as they rode together in the back seat. Jonas was humming and checking email or texting, still smelling freshly showered despite the restaurant.

Lord, he wanted... no. No wanting. Jonas was fancy, and they had a working thing and.... Well, maybe a little looking.

The car pulled up, and Jonas paid with an app, then climbed out onto the sidewalk. "Your box of stuff should already be in the ward, probably at the nurses' station. I'll check when we get up there. You ready?"

"Yes, sir. I'm on it."

"Remember, some of the kids are very ill."

Sterling rolled his eyes. "I got it."

Jonas sighed. "I've heard that before." They got in an elevator and stepped off on the fifth floor. The cheerful colors and art on the walls made it immediately clear that it was a pediatric ward. There were Christmas decorations still up everywhere too—garland and spray-on snow on the windows and stockings hanging on the walls. The nurses' station had a little Santa sitting on the counter with his legs down a chimney, and a menorah on the other end all lit up.

The social worker came up to him with a huge smile. "Mister Kingsolver?"

"Sterling, ma'am. Please. I'm tickled to be here."

"Sterling. I'm Belinda Martinez. The children are very excited to meet a real cowboy."

"I'm very excited to meet all of them. Do you have a mask for me to wear under my bandana for the at-risk kiddos?" He knew the healthier kids would meet him in the common room, but the others would each have special needs.

He ignored the curious look from Jonas in favor of the bright smile he got from Belinda. "We do! I'll bring you one. We've got a little crew in the rec lounge ready to meet you, so why don't we start you there, and then we'll get you cleaned up so you can stop in on everyone else."

"Yes, ma'am. I can't wait." He couldn't stop smiling. For the first time since he got off the plane, he felt like he knew what to do. He just needed to answer questions, give hugs where they were wanted, and tell stories about being a cowboy in the Wild West.

9

Jonas fell into step behind them, listening to Sterling chat with Belinda and ask her all kinds of excited questions about the kids as they made their way down the long hall. Whatever else was going on, Sterling had obviously done this before, because the cowboy seemed to know what was up, and he could tell by the swing in Sterling's shoulders as they walked that the man was more relaxed than he'd been since they'd met.

"You have hats and bandanas in the room to give out."

"Excellent. I'll make sure they can have them if they want. I don't want to stress anyone out. Hats can be real weird, I know."

How on earth did he know that?

Belinda hooked her arm around Sterling's back and gave a quick squeeze. "We're going to like you around here, Sterling. It really helps to have someone visit who gets it. Last week, our Santa was cute but a little too timid." She stopped them just shy of the rec room; he knew because he could hear the kids inside. "I'll follow you in, and I'll be in the room the whole time you're here." She looked at Jonas. "You're Mister Burke?"

"Yeah. Jonas is fine."

"Are you coming in with us, Jonas?"

"I'd like to, if it's okay." What was he going to do, stand in the hall?

"Just checking. The last guy from your agency was a little awkward around children." She smiled at him. "I'm here if you need me."

He didn't know a damn thing about kids, actually, but he was staying with Sterling.

Belinda gestured to the door. "Go on in whenever you're ready, Sterling."

Sterling knocked on the door, then opened it up, all smiles. "Hey, y'all. Has anybody seen my horse? I got bucked off, and she took off running."

Before Jonas could blink, Sterling was sitting on the floor, telling one story after another. There were two kids on Sterling's lap, nearly everyone had hats on, and they were all singing some ridiculous song.

He didn't need to worry about entertaining kids himself, after all, because every single one of them was gathered around Sterling. Some of them were dressed, some in gowns, a couple were bald-headed, but they were all smiling. He leaned on a wall and watched the biggest kid of all, right in the middle, trying to reconcile that sight with the guy with the split lip he'd seen leaning on the bar the night before.

"He's something else," Belinda said, leaning on the wall next to him.

"He's... yeah. Something else." Sterling looked completely at home in this room, in his skin, kind of the way he'd looked in his beat-up jeans. Comfortable. Adorable.

She looked at him. "He seems like a sweetheart."

Jonas felt himself squint. "He does seem that way, doesn't he?"

"A little bit. A lot of the time these guys are stiff and nervous, and the children react to that. Sterling is acting like this is normal."

A young man with Down syndrome came to Sterling, obviously telling him a story, and Sterling listened to every word, looking interested, not like he was waiting for the rambling tale to be finished.

He was smiling too, he knew, at everything—at Sterling's patience, at the kids. At that young man who felt safe enough to talk to a cowboy.

There was no way in hell, were Cody Ball in Sterling's shoes today, that this would be going so well. Cody loved the cameras and the show, and it seemed like the guy knew how to put on a good one. That had its place too, but not here. Sterling was just... real. And to think, if Jonas had been fired, he'd have missed this.

"I'm going to get him moving to see a few of the other children. I'm afraid we're going to blow your schedule...." Belinda didn't sound terribly upset by that fact.

Sterling wouldn't be either. Jonas looked over at Belinda and smiled. "We're not in any rush. Sterling specifically asked me how long he would get to stay. Obviously he enjoys this."

Obviously, right? They had nothing else on the calendar for today. They could take their time. After yesterday, maybe the cowboy needed some of this. He wasn't about to rush Sterling out.

"Okay, children. Tell Sterling goodbye. He's going to go visit some of the children who couldn't come to play."

There were some tears, and Sterling told every single

parent and child goodbye before they slipped out into the hallway again.

Belinda handed them both masks and stopped at the nurses' station where she asked Sterling to wash up.

"You really like kids." Jonas watched, noticing how Sterling's smile softened those dark eyes.

"I do, yeah. Very much." Sterling scrubbed his hands, then put on his paper mask. "Bandana or not? I can tie it around my neck and just see how they do?"

Belinda looked Sterling over. "They're used to the masks, so maybe not at first, and then you can pull it on if they seem into it. Sound good? A couple of them are older. Tracy is thirteen, and Ben, if he's awake, is almost sixteen. Are you okay with them too?"

"Sure. I took care of my sister, Grace, and she made it to adulthood. No worries."

"No wonder you're a natural. Grace is lucky to have you. Come on. Everyone knows you're coming, so you won't startle anybody. Harris first. Room 521. I'm right behind you."

Sterling had a sick sister? He'd like to ask, but not now. Maybe later over a beer. The guy deserved a beer.

One room after another, Sterling did his thing, talking and laughing. One little girl asked him to pray for her, another wanted to see pictures of his horse, which Sterling totally had on his phone.

Ben, the older boy Belinda mentioned, wasn't awake, but his mom was there, and she got some pictures of her sleeping son with the cowboy and seemed really grateful Sterling had come by.

Sterling had a huge heart and all this... compassion, and Jonas was really kind of awed by how much more there was to the cowboy than just a bull riding championship. He doubted the league would be as impressed, but they should be.

Finally, well after lunchtime, they were shaking Belinda's hand, the social worker singing Sterling's praises.

"Thank you so much for coming out."

"Oh, ma'am. It was my pleasure. I had a ball. Everyone was amazing." Sterling beamed, but Jonas thought he looked tired around the edges.

"I took a few pictures with my phone. Can I send them to you so you can get permission from parents in case the league wants to use a couple?"

He really didn't feel like talking business after such a great day, but that's what he was here for. Belinda agreed and saw them into an elevator.

He looked over at Sterling as soon as the doors closed. "Coffee? Beer? Nap?"

"Beer. Food? I'm hungry as all get-out."

"I know a great place. We'll get you those fries you didn't get last night." Man, was that only last night? It was hard to believe this was the same guy standing next to him in the elevator.

He let Sterling recharge his batteries on the ride over and didn't say much while he checked his email and set up rides for tomorrow's PR session, but once they were seated in his favorite burger joint with beers ordered, he put his phone away and smiled at the cowboy.

"You okay? That took some energy, so you must be tired."

"Just a bit; mostly I'm good. That was fun." Sterling smiled at him, the lines beside his dark eyes crinkling up. "Seriously, that was great. So many neat kids, and they were all on their best behavior."

"You were exceptional with them. I... I was surprised."

Was that okay to say? Damn. But the kids just loved Sterling, and he'd had such a one-sided experience with the cowboy so far.

"Yeah? I'm pretty much a white hat, I think. Usually. Sometimes I'm a butthead, I guess, but I try to do the right thing."

"You haven't done anything wrong since I picked you up at the airport, you know. I mean, work is work, but separate that out? You're...."

Beautiful.

Fuck, where was that beer?

"A cowboy, scars and all." Now that was sure, confident, happy, and hot as hell.

God, he could....

But he wouldn't because Sterling was a cowboy. Sterling was his paycheck. Sterling was leaving town in four days, and there would be no reason for their lives to intersect ever again. One thing he knew about himself was that he was fine with one-night stands, but once that included breakfast, he was hopeless. He dove in with both feet every time.

And he didn't own cowboy boots.

"You do have a few scars, don't you? I noticed the one big one when you...." He'd seen muscle too. A lot of muscle. And tan. "You know, where's that beer?"

"The big one was from a four-wheeler when I was thirteen. There was an arroyo that I didn't see in time, and I went ass over teakettle." Sterling rolled his eyes, grinned.

"Arroyo?"

"A piece of the desert that's carved out by water. They got steep sides and can be damn deep. They can run for a good ways."

"Oh crap." Jonas picked up his beer the second their server set it down. "That had to hurt."

"Like a motherfucker. I was lucky. Ripped myself wide open and broke my ankle, but that was it." Sterling picked up his glass and drank deep.

"That was it?" He laughed. "Just ripped myself wide open, no big deal. I'm a cowboy." He couldn't help but tease.

"Exactly. You begin to understand." Sterling's eyes danced with mischief. "So tell me, how does a person end up doing your job?"

"They have no sense of self-worth, so they need to live vicariously through people with fame and fortune." He gave Sterling his best toothy grin. "Or so I'm told."

"Look at you, Mister Teeth." Sterling winked at him. "Do you like it? I can't imagine what it's like, having to deal with so many different people."

"I am good at it. I like people, I like personalities, and I like a well-oiled machine. I'm kind of compulsively organized. I like when I work hard to make something happen and it comes off so smoothly you'd never know it was hard." He was great at running, being busy, juggling.

He looked at Sterling, took another big swig of his beer, and then grinned. "Usually celebrities are experienced. Cooperative. Predictable. You, sir, are none of those things. Not a single one."

"I cooperated, now. I did all the things you told me to yesterday." Sterling stuck his tongue out, wrinkled his nose.

"Okay. You did them, yes. But you offered to take the interviewer snipe hunting, man, which I thought was cute until her assistant googled it." She'd been a little condescending, sure, but that might have been uncalled for.

"Well, you know... I was trying to make friends. At least I didn't tell her to watch out for the cucuy."

He eyed Sterling and pulled out his phone. Bogeyman. Sort of. "Funny. Anyway, you didn't make a friend there."

"I'm beginning to think that I'm not making friends anywhere anymore."

"Well, you could say that's not really your job, I guess." It did sound like Sterling was losing people left and right. He reached over and gave Sterling's hand a squeeze. "You just need to get through the week, right?"

"Right." Sterling pinked and shrugged, thumb just barely stroking his knuckle before disappearing.

He blinked and gently pulled his hand back. Reaching for Sterling had been impulsive, but he didn't regret it. He caught the cowboy's eyes and shrugged back. "You'll get through it. I read one article that said your run this year was historic. And I guess if that doesn't work out for you, you can get a job visiting kids in hospitals in your cowboy hat."

"Yeah. I will." Sterling closed his eyes, and for a second, the man looked lost, young, and then the expression was gone.

"Sterling—"

Their burgers arrived, interrupting him. Jonas sighed and leaned back as they were set down, huge plates with fries and pickles. A big bottle of ketchup landed between them.

"Another beer?" their server asked.

He gestured to Sterling. "Yeah. Him too, please."

She nodded and hurried off.

"Looks great. Thank you." Sterling fell on the food like a starving man, devouring the hamburger.

He wanted to know what was so awful. He wanted to know why this cowboy's issues seemed bigger than one pissed-off second-place finisher. He wanted to know what was weighing so heavily on Sterling's shoulders.

There were other things he wanted to know about Sterling too, like how that scar felt under his fingers.

He watched the cowboy's burger start to disappear, and he had to grin—the guy really knew how to eat.

Finally, Sterling slowed down, possibly tasting the food. Maybe. "Oh. Oh, man. I was wanting me some of that."

"Yeah, looks like it." He laughed and picked up his burger, took a big bite, nodding at Sterling. "Good." When he finished chewing, he added, "I love this place. So much food."

"Sometimes you got to feed your hunger, buddy, huh?" Sterling started in on his fries.

He chuckled and took a sip of his beer. He wasn't touching that with a ten-foot pole. Despite the giant burger in front of him, he was starting to feel like a starving man.

God, he could watch Sterling eat french fries for months. The man wasn't just eating—he was fellating them.

"You... like those fries." Jesus. It was going to be a long, and hard, few days.

"Salty. Sweet. Crispy. What's not to like?"

"Yep. Delicious." He was suddenly all out of small talk. Just... done. His pulse was up, and his jeans felt like a prison. His brain wasn't supplying anything useful for conversation. He looked down at his plate and tried a french fry, but it wasn't the least bit satisfying.

Shit, he was in big trouble.

"You okay? You look all stressed out." Sterling stared at him, brows furrowed. "You want something else? Onion rings? Fried cheese?"

He laughed. "No. No, I'm good. I'm just full."

Ice water. Polar ice caps. Penguins? Mrs. Jones, my third grade teacher with the big mole on her nose. Ew, that was so gross. Oh. Unemployment.

Unemployment was so not sexy.

"Okay. Well, we can go, whenever you want." Sterling

gave him a sheepish look. "I don't suppose they'd give me a doggy bag for your fries? For tonight?"

He grinned. "Yeah. They will." Jonas waved the server over and got the check and a doggy bag. A few more deep breaths and he was feeling more like he could walk home without embarrassing himself. Damn. It had been a while since he'd felt like that.

He scooped his fries into the box, stuck the box into the goodie bag, and handed it to Sterling. "One midnight snack."

"Thanks. I get the munchies." Like Sterling couldn't just dial room service.

"You ready?" They'd walk back. This place was a hike from the hospital but just a few blocks from the hotel. He stood up and turned around to get his coat on, making sure he wasn't still busting through his jeans, but things seemed fairly under control. Thank God. When he turned back, he gave Sterling a smile. "You're free until tomorrow."

"Oh, right." Sterling looked a bit disappointed, but he simply nodded once. "Okay. Thank you. Can you please point me to the hotel?"

"Oh, I'm walking back with you, no worries. You're not supposed to be out of my sight, remember?" He let himself believe for one second that the disappointment had to do with him. Just a second. Or maybe a whole minute. Maybe he'd just let himself believe it for a while later, alone in his hotel room.

Jesus, look at that smile. It could light up the entire street. "Do you...? Which way do we go?"

Yes, I do. He pointed up the sidewalk and started walking. "North. Three blocks. And then one block east." But if he'd read the man right, Sterling wasn't ready to call it a day. "Unless... well. You're probably tired."

"Unless what?" Sterling kept up easily.

"Well, I don't know. You want to go out? What do you like to do for fun?"

"All sorts of things. I ride four-wheelers. I ski and snowmobile. Play a lot of cards." Sterling began to laugh. "I go sing karaoke."

"You sing?" He laughed along. No one was four-wheeling in Manhattan, but karaoke bars were popular. "I wonder if I can find a Western bar that does karaoke?"

"I do! It's goofy, but it's fun. Have you ever tried it? Karaoke?"

"No. I'm more of a behind-the-scenes guy, you know?" He was googling, though, as they walked. Seeing what he could find. "Nothing wrong with goofy. I'm into a good laugh. It beats bowling, which was my next suggestion."

"We bowl a lot at the casinos at home. Not so much on the road."

He stopped walking to get a better look at his phone. "Found a bar in Boho. They have George Strait on their song list, so we're probably good, yeah?" He grinned at Sterling. Go him. Cowboy karaoke. He rocked this job.

"Yeah? You want to?" Look at that—lit up and excited, eager and animated. If Sterling could do that on camera, the man would be famous. He didn't care much about the camera right now, though, he just wanted to see more of that smile for himself. He still couldn't believe this was the same guy.

"Yeah. Sounds like fun. I sang in a choir once, maybe I can still carry a tune." Doubtful, but another beer and he really wouldn't care. He stepped over to the curb and held a hand up, and they had a cab in a couple of minutes. "I didn't ask if you wanted to change first. Are you comfy? You want to stop by the hotel?"

"I'm golden. I got my boots, I washed the sizing off the shirt, and I've got my good coat. It's colder at home, but the wind whips around the buildings, huh?"

He gave the cabbie the address and got settled in the back seat. "Totally. The wind just never stops. Comes right off the river, so it's extra icy. Once you live here a while, you realize that scarves and earmuffs are more than just accessories."

"Yeah. My granny made me a super-thin thing that you can wear under your hat and it covers your ears. Love it."

"Do you have a lot of family? I heard you mention your sister at the hospital."

"There's just me and Grace and the folks. I have a shit-ton of cousins and stuff, but there's just us. My land butts up to Daddy's, so together we have five hundred acres."

"Whoa. What do you do with all that land?" He grew up on half an acre. At the moment he had a five-hundred-square-foot apartment that he didn't even own. He couldn't even fathom what five hundred acres looked like.

"Cattle, horses. Momma has alpacas and chickens and goats." Sterling grinned over as the cab lurched along. "I'm going to invest in bison. I think they'll make some money."

"Wow. I don't think I know what a bison looks like." He googled. God, he was looking up so much shit you'd think Sterling lived in a foreign country. Cattle, bison, he couldn't imagine what it was like to live like that. *Starbucks anyone?* A picture popped up, and he nodded. "Oh, yeah. That's a bison."

The cab jerked to a stop, and he paid the driver.

"Beefalo and stuff are all the rage." Sterling knew how to talk about things he wanted to, didn't he?

"Beefalo?" Beefalo. That he could guess at. He followed Sterling out of the cab. "Cross-bred cows and buffalo?

Why are they all the rage?" Newfangled livestock. Who knew?

"Well, bison is super lean, right? But they're not domesticable and...."

Listen to that. Who knew there was so much to know about cows and buffalo?

He listened and he tried to get it, he really did. But man, he just didn't speak that language. He let Sterling go on until the cowboy wound down a little. The bar was covered in Christmas lights and garland, a raggedy, fake tree in the corner by the little karaoke stage. "Shot of something?" He bumped shoulders with Sterling, herding him over to the bar.

"I would like a... you know what? I would. I'll take a shot of Cuervo, I think. What's your poison?"

"I'm in. And beer chasers, and then we'll have a look at their song list." The bar wasn't too crowded. It was early in the evening, so there were seats to be had, and he got a seat with a good view of the stage. The stage featured a couple of mics on stands and was lit with concert-style lighting. "This is kind of neat. I rarely go places I've never been before in this city. I thought I'd done it all."

"Well, look at that. I helped you find something new." Sterling beamed. "This bar seems way nicer than last night's...."

He laughed. "Last night's was the perfect setting for a bar fight. Well done." This one was cozy and in the West Village. They might try to outsing each other, but no one was going to fight.

Two shots and two beers landed on the bar, along with a dish of limes and a salt shaker.

Sterling grabbed his wallet and paid for the drinks. "This round's on me, not the league."

He looked over at Sterling and smiled, the gesture not lost on him. Not at all. "I will enjoy it that much more, then. Thanks." He picked up the salt shaker, feeling Sterling watch him lick his hand and sprinkle salt on it.

Sterling grabbed his lime and did the same, then lifted his shot. "Cheers, buddy."

He looked right into those dark eyes, so dark they stood out even in the bar lighting, and touched his shot to Sterling's. "Here's to a good day." He knocked it back, the burn making him shiver, and stuffed his lime into his mouth.

Sterling hummed, taking his time biting into his lime, gaze heavy as a touch on him.

That look.

He swallowed. Somebody liked tequila. Yeah, that was the tequila. He returned the look, popping the lime out of his mouth so he could smile.

The back of his hand tingled where Sterling's thumb had run over it at dinner. Without that, he might not be sure about the cowboy, but he was damn sure now. He knew better than to think about a client this way, but dammit, how often was he going to find a hot, tan, muscled-up cowboy who was interested in him? It was like some crazy fantasy.

Plus, it was just a few days. How attached could he get? It's not like he had anything to offer that Sterling would be interested in. Other than sex. He was good at that. He could totally rope a cowboy into bed.

First, though, he wanted to see the unassuming, stoic cowboy sing.

Sterling laughed, the sound wrapping around him, drawing him closer. "Man, that is a great burn. Tequila is a magical animal."

Then, in a move that was smooth as glass, Sterling

picked up his beer and wrapped callused fingers around his wrist. "Come help me pick a song?"

"You got it." He grabbed his beer and got tugged along, grinning and sharing Sterling's enthusiasm. He couldn't wait to hear the guy sing. They grabbed seats at a table close to the stage and flipped through a huge book. "What do you usually do?"

"I like Brad Paisley, Keith Urban, some Garth. I've done a couple Chris Stapleton, but he's a challenge. You have to belt it, huh?"

He laughed. "My mom is a Willie Nelson fan. That's about all I know about country music."

"My daddy is too. He's a Texan, through and through." Sterling ran his hand down one of the lists. "What about you? You gonna sing or no?"

His mom was not a Texan; she was from Rochester. But Willie was this universal presence, and had been as long as he could remember.

"If you promise not to laugh too hard, I'll sing." What? Sing? Him? Why did he say that? What the hell was he going to sing? "You pick, and then I'll look at the book while you wait."

"I'll do something fun, then, to start." Sterling picked "Ticks," then went to put his name on the list.

There was a song called "Ticks"? Oh, that oughta be good. He pulled the book over and started flipping through. Something fun, right? After settling on the Eagles, he went and put his name in too, and then joined Sterling back at the bar.

Sterling didn't seem nervous, looking at his phone, texting. When Jonas sat down, Sterling looked up and grinned. "I have a new foal. Want to see?"

Sterling held out his phone, the picture one of a spindly

legged tiny horse, a smiling woman who had to be Sterling's mom, and a young lady with Down syndrome.

He took the phone and spent a minute looking at the picture. "Cute little thing. That's your mom, right? Has to be. You look just like her. And is that Grace?" He handed the phone back, smiling. "Good-looking family."

"Thank you. This is her first foal. Momma said everything went all right." Sterling looked so pleased.

"I'm sorry you missed it." It wasn't the same as a baby or anything, but it seemed important to Sterling.

"There will be more." Sterling winked at him, playfully. "Truthfully, the whole miracle-of-life thing has a relatively high gross factor."

"Ew. I'll pass, then." Jonas laughed and sipped his beer.

"Sterling? Oh, that's a great name. Where's Sterling? You're on deck." The DJ waved at them.

"You're up next!" He grinned wide. "Break a leg!"

"I'm on it." Sterling strutted up to the stage, completely unafraid, and it made Jonas's mouth dry, the walk and the way those jeans molded to a tight, tiny ass.

Then Sterling took the microphone and began to sing.

Okay, that was surprising—Sterling's singing voice was rich and clear, confident.

He sipped his beer and laughed at the lyrics, but really he was most impressed with Sterling's stage presence, the smile so easy now there weren't any cameras.

The little crowd hooted and hollered, applauding, and Sterling took a bow.

He was so happy for Sterling, and he didn't even know why. Jonas just felt like the guy had worries and didn't deserve them, even if he didn't know what they were.

He applauded like everyone else, including one overt

catcall, and laughed as Sterling made his way back to the bar. "That was amazing! You're so good!"

"Thank you, thank you." That was a dramatic bow and a bright smile.

Two more shots hit the bar, and the bartender grinned at Sterling. "On the house, cowboy. You hit the top of the applause meter."

Sterling beamed, then bowed. "Well, thank you sir. I appreciate it." Sterling handed him one of the shots. "Not bad, huh?"

"Good, in fact. Not bad. Really good. How come you can do that, but you can't smile for a camera?" He picked up his shot and held it up.

Sterling rolled his eyes, tossed back his shot. "I was miserable yesterday, man. The shirt itched, the boots hurt, the jeans didn't fit right. Then I had to stress fucking the goo on my face up."

Jonas swallowed his shot and sucked on the lime. So good. He did like tequila. He was just about to tell Sterling that they were going to have another day like that on Thursday when his name was called.

"Jonas? You're on deck!"

"Oh shit." He put down his lime, took a quick sip of his beer, and looked at Sterling. "No funny faces, I'll lose it." He winked and headed for the stage, but he didn't have half Sterling's swagger. The only reason he wasn't shaking was the tequila had given him some nerve.

He'd gone for fun, because that was what Sterling suggested. He didn't give himself a chance to back out or panic. He just grabbed the mic and gave the DJ a nod.

Sterling watched him like a hawk, and he swore that dark gaze dragged over every inch of him. Damn.

The crowd applauded and laughed as the music began, and it was a good thing, because Sterling had him a little distracted. He came in late on the first line but caught up fast, and was feeling much more relaxed by the time he hit the chorus of "Heartache Tonight." Yeah. Had to be the tequila.

When the crowd started singing along, it was a huge rush. Almost as good as when he finished and Sterling stood up and gave him a standing ovation.

He gave the audience a quick, embarrassed bow, handed the mic back, and laughed himself off the stage, shaking his head all the way back to the bar. He waved Sterling off. "Yeah, yeah. Sit down." He chuckled and slid onto his barstool.

"You did great! You're brave." Sterling laughed, but it wasn't at him—it was with him.

"Or stupid. It was fun, though. Nerve-wracking, but fun. I didn't hurl." He picked up his beer and took a huge gulp, willing away the adrenaline rush. It didn't work. "I'm glad I didn't pick a ballad. You'd have heard me shaking."

"You did fine. It was all cool. Seriously." Sterling leaned back in his chair and grinned at him.

He shrugged. It hadn't been so awful. He was still sober enough to know he'd at least hit the notes and hadn't been laughed at. He let his eyes wander over Sterling's face and licked his lips. "Thanks. Are you going up again?"

"Yeah, if you have time. I'd like to try another."

He nodded and watched as Sterling put another song on the list. He had all evening. Maybe all night if the cowboy was into it, and if he laid off the tequila. Whoa. He could watch Sterling walk around in those jeans on stage or off. No problem.

"All set?" he asked when Sterling got back. The woman up there singing now was fantastic, and she was practically channeling Madonna. "So while we're waiting for you to blow us all away again, tell me more about Grace."

"She's my baby sister—fourteen months younger than me, so I don't remember not having her around. She works at the feed store part-time, and she has a casita of her own that she loves." Sterling loved her, it was obvious, and was proud of her. "Of course, she's not too fond of the dark, so she has a bedroom at my folks' house and at mine."

"She sounds great, and you seem like a very fond big brother. She's lucky to have you. I got a couple of pictures of you singing 'Ticks.' I'll send them to you so you can send them to her." She probably missed Sterling, even though he must be gone a fair amount with all the riding.

"That would tickle the shit out of her. I called her this morning before she left for work. She was very excited to know if things here were all apples."

He laughed. "You'll have to get her a Big Apple souvenir. There are snow globes and other tacky but neat things. I'll drag you by a gift shop in Midtown at some point."

"I'd love that. I got the family and my traveling partner to get things for."

"Who's your traveling partner? Is that uh... Chance, was it?" What did Sterling say he did? "The big show guy? Not that I have any idea what that is." Mars. These cowboys might as well be Martians.

"Yeah. Chance Leonards. He rides with me. He's a shit bull rider, but the fans love him, so he's still around. Good man. I like him and Bobby both."

"Bobby? Another bull rider?" He had to wonder if any of these guys were lovers or just guys. And then he had to wonder why he was wondering. Damn.

"Bobby was a team roper, but he got hurt, so he went to work their ranch."

"Oh. Bummer. I guess that must happen a lot. What I've seen looks crazy dangerous." What it looked like was a really hard way to make a living.

"Yeah, men have died. Chance was real scared, but Bobby came through." Sterling didn't sound like Chance and Bobby were just buds. Not a bit.

He nodded, just to let Sterling know he got it. "I'm glad for them." And that simplified things for him too.

"Sterling! You're up!" The DJ waved a mic at them, and people were already cheering.

He huffed out a laugh, squinting at the cowboy. "Your fans are waiting."

"You know it." Sterling bowed dramatically and ran to the stage. This time the cowboy belted out some blues song, and damn, Sterling's voice was this hot mix of rough and velvety at once and it just settled right into him, made him hard.

He was so done thinking. From here on out, he was flirting instead.

The final notes rang out, filling the air, and Sterling stared at him, gaze burning into him.

The bar went bananas, interrupting the moment, but not before he'd had a chance to return Sterling's look with a shallow nod. Then he was on his feet, applauding with everyone else. He kept his eyes on Sterling's as long as he could, and then he drained the rest of his beer.

Sterling's cheeks were rosy, and there was no telling whether it was him, the booze, or the applause, but it was him Sterling came to.

He sucked in a breath as Sterling got just a step closer than he'd anticipated. "That was—" *Hot. So fucking hot.* "—amazing."

"Thanks." Sterling held his gaze, so sure of himself, desire burning between them. "Hotel?"

He swallowed and nodded, Sterling's confidence making him ache, making him need. Jonas reached back and pulled his coat off the back of his barstool. "Ready."

Sterling shrugged into his coat, and they headed out. Jonas swore he could feel the electricity between them. He thought maybe everyone else could too, with the way that they seemed to part the crowd.

The cold air surrounded them as Sterling hustled him out the door, but it barely touched him. It might as well have been a cool breeze on a spring afternoon. "Just need a cab." He headed for the curb and held up a hand.

"You from here, or did you come here on purpose?"

Did Sterling just touch his ass?

"I'm uh...." The pause was so he could flag a cab down. That's what he was going with. It didn't have anything to do with trying to catch his breath. "I'm from upstate originally. Then Mom moved us to Jersey City. I moved into the city for school and then stayed for work."

"Cool. I got my degree online at ENMU. Worked out good."

The cab pulled up, and Sterling reached around to open the door for him. He smiled as he got in, startled but pleased.

"What's your degree in?" Did you need a degree in bull riding?

"Agricultural business."

That was a thing?

"Oh. So you can run your farm? I swear, it's like you're from another planet sometimes. I say that respectfully. It's just that some of the things you talk about are so out of my... experience. I feel like an idiot." He laughed, because he wasn't an idiot, but he'd never felt so mystified by anyone before.

Sterling grinned over, shook his head. "I'm glad I've traveled some. I know I seem like a yokel, but at least I've been around. I can tell you, where I come from, it's different."

"No. No, it's not like that." He took one of Sterling's hands. "Not at all. You can get really jaded doing what I do, all the picky little demands, the busy schedules, the money. You were just... unexpected."

"Well, thank you. Just think, you were fixin' to give up on me last night."

"I didn't say you were easy." He winked at Sterling. "You, Cody and his fucking posse, this stupid league that wants a cowboy to look like he's never seen dirt. It's the fucking holidays. You're too much work."

"Tell me they're paying out the ass for you, at least."

"Mmm... no." He snorted and shook his head. "Let's just say that this assignment wasn't something I could afford to turn down." He could feel Sterling's calluses and flipped the cowboy's hand over so he could see them and run his fingers over them. "You work harder than I do."

"I work with my hands more than you do. I've watched you work." Oh, the compliment felt so damn good. If he blushed any harder he might burst into flames.

Sterling's hands felt good in his. Warm, solid, strangely gentle for all their calluses and strength. Definitely steadier than he was, but they grounded him a little, and he wanted the contact. "Almost there."

"Good." That single word filled with so much meaning, but it was the squeeze, the way Sterling's fingers curled over his palms to touch him, that made him ache.

The silence that filled the cab after that wasn't awkward

at all, but it was uncomfortable, both of them wanting more than they had right now. He was in a hurry and not, wanting everything but not all at once, so he didn't try to maul the cowboy here in the taxi, as tempting as that was.

When the cab stopped outside their hotel, he handed over cash and stuffed the receipt in his pocket.

They didn't speak until they got out of the elevator—what small talk did they need to use? But as soon as they got down the hall, Sterling leaned, bumping their shoulders together. "Does it matter which room?"

He leaned back, grinning. "Our rooms adjoin, but yours is five feet closer, and I don't have any Dr Pepper."

"Well, then. Come on in." Sterling opened the door and let him in, setting his hat down on the little table by the door. The room looked just the same, except now Sterling was right up against him, solid and muscled, gaze holding his.

"Oh fuck." He grabbed Sterling by the shoulders and ran his hands down and over muscles like he'd never had his hands on before. Then he leaned in slowly, breathing Sterling in.

"I'm all over that." Sterling wrapped one hand around his nape and brought their lips together. No hesitation, no clumsy fumbling—Sterling knew what he was doing.

Oh, bring it on.

Jonas opened for Sterling, loving how their tongues slid together. Sterling tasted like tequila and smelled like a man should, and whatever jitters Jonas had left just melted away. He couldn't quite tangle his fingers in the cowboy's hair, but he liked mussing it, sliding his fingers through it.

Sterling's moan buzzed his lips as Sterling pushed up, deepening their kiss until he could barely breathe.

He went for Sterling's shirt, fingers working the snaps

easily before tugging it free of the waistband of Sterling's jeans. He broke their kiss, not just to get a breath but to look, to watch his fingers slide over all that tan skin and tough muscle. Sterling's nipples were tight and hard, the ridged muscle of that belly like a playground.

He traced along the valleys with his fingers, fascinated, feeling them move as the cowboy breathed. Then he reached up and pushed the shirt off Sterling's shoulders so he could go after a nipple with each of his thumbs, letting himself be curious, wanting to make Sterling *feel*. React.

Sterling shrugged his shirt and coat off, before pushing Jonas's coat to the floor. The motion made Sterling's pec leap under his fingers.

"God." He let his coat fall and took another kiss, undoing his buttons and dragging his shirt off as well. He was growing impatient, fingers itching for more skin, mouth hungry for Sterling's. They met, skin-on-skin, and Sterling rubbed all along his body, hands splayed out on his back.

He could feel Sterling hard against his hip, and Jonas moaned, rocking forward. "You feel good."

Sterling's answer was a low, musical moan that sounded right before one hot hand cupped his ass.

He pinched Sterling's lip between his teeth and tugged on it, rocking between the hand searing through his jeans and grinding their pricks together. "More?"

"Fuck yes." Sterling pulled him to the bed. "I'm gonna take off my boots before we get too hard and heavy."

Practical cowboy.

He grinned. "Okay." He kicked off his shoes and tugged his socks off with them, then gave Sterling a playful shove onto the bed and knelt. "I'll help."

"Ooh. Sexy." Sterling's warm smile belied his teasing words. "Ooh a la, you're fine, no?"

"I'm fine. But you're hot." He winked and tugged one boot off, then went after the other.

"Thank you." Sterling curled down, kissing him again, hand behind his head, drawing him up onto Sterling's lap.

He settled on the bed, straddling Sterling's thighs. Sterling's kisses felt so deliberate, so in control. He wanted to make it a goal to frazzle the cowboy a little. He crawled forward on his knees until they were tucked close together and sucked hard on Sterling's tongue.

Sterling jerked, humping up into him, both of them almost leaving the bed.

He dropped his hands between them, and tugged on Sterling's belt buckle, willing it to loosen up, but his fingers failed him. "Fuck." He was so hard his jeans were strangling him. He groaned, giving up on Sterling's buckle and tore open his own instead.

"Good." Sterling whipped his belt open, his fly, exposing a hard, thick bulge in his tighty-whities.

"Yeah. That's it." Fuck, Jonas wanted a taste of that. He looked into those dark eyes, stared into them and licked his lips, brushing his fingers over the thin fabric. Sterling's head snapped back at the touch, the expression desperate and wanton and open.

"Oh Jesus. Look at you." He'd never seen anything, anyone like that. Just... that honest. He shifted off Sterling's lap and hooked his fingers into a belt loop, tugging. "Get these off. Come on."

"Uh-huh. Damn. You too." Sterling stripped down, giving him one hell of a view. Cock hard and full, belly flat and taut, and that ass....

He kicked his jeans off, so focused on Sterling that he hissed in surprise as the fabric slid over his own swollen prick. "Shit." He laughed softly as he swore. "Look how you've got me."

"Mm-hmm...." Sterling reached out and cupped his cock, the pressure firm enough to make his eyes cross. He made a strangled sound that he'd meant to be words and braced himself on Sterling's shoulder, leaning in for another kiss and wrapping his fingers around the cowboy's thick erection.

Sterling's cry pushed into his lips, the sound echoed by the pressure of those callused fingers squeezing him tight. Sterling didn't give him a bit of quarter, the man jacking him like there was nothing on earth he'd rather be doing.

He leaned into Sterling, tangling their legs as they fell back into bed. He tried to concentrate, to slow Sterling down, but those calluses and the need in their kiss kept shorting him out. Fuck, it felt good. Instead, he gave as good as he got, pumping and adding pressure to the head of Sterling's cock on each stroke.

"Jesus. Get the edge off, then we'll go again, hmm?" Oh, Sterling was proving to have the best ideas.

He nodded and arched into those determined fingers, impressed that the man could think that clearly, let alone speak. Neither of them had much to say after that, though. The hotel room filled with heavy panting and long moans as Jonas let himself get lost in a kiss as deep as the ocean.

At some point Sterling took them both in hand, arm working like a piston. He was trying not to drown under the waves of their hungry kisses. There wasn't much hope of holding out for long, though. A howl ripped through him as he came with a shudder, everything about it a little chaotic and out of control. He held on to Sterling as his vision narrowed, fingers digging in anywhere they could. Sterling followed right behind, his heat joining Jonas's, the cowboy jerking wildly against him.

They lay there, taking in each other's breaths, hands hovering over sensitive areas, sticky fingers tangling together until one of them chuckled, the other huffed out a laugh, and both of them collapsed back, giggling like kids.

He grinned over at Sterling, whose face was red and forehead damp. "Holy shit, cowboy. What the fuck was that?"

"Sex, honey. That was sex. What do they teach y'all up here?"

He laughed and pinched one of Sterling's nipples. "Smartass. That wasn't sex. That was like, high school, out behind the gym, sneaky hand jobs. I'll show you what they teach us up here. Just give me a few minutes."

"Dude, y'all had better high schools, then."

That set them off again, both of them holding on to each other, howling.

"Fuck, I feel good. I'd been working up to that since... wait. Has it only been two days? Damn!" He was still giggling. Two days. Jesus.

"We have to work fast. Remember, I get my work week done in eight seconds."

Oh damn. Cute.

"If you did this for the cameras...."

"Then how I am with you isn't as good." This time, it was less teasing, more warm.

"Well, at least I'm doing my job." He rolled up on his side and slid a hand over those hard abs. "I'm not letting you out of my sight."

10

They didn't just order room service—they had a goddamn feast. Pasta and bacon and eggs and spicy chicken sandwiches and tacos and three full orders of french fries.

Sterling was naked as the day he was born, feeding Jonas bites of taco, licking his fingers free of sour cream and salsa.

This was fun as fuck.

Even if he was sore in some rare goddamn places. Lord, they'd tore each other up.

"I thought bull riders were like jockeys. Don't you have to watch your weight?" Jonas nipped at one of his fingers.

"Yep. I got two weeks before I have to stress that. When I hit fourteen days before I ride, I eat nothing but chicken breasts and eggs." He had that shit down to a fine art. He knew how to shave those five pounds off.

Jonas picked up his Coke and tangled their fingers together. "Don't you worry you're going to get hurt? Like really hurt, like your friend?"

"Now? Yeah." Sterling squeezed his fingers. Without the

bullfighters, the safety men, he was in trouble. He'd have to see if he could figure out who was on his side.

"Now. You mean now that you won? Does Cody have that much influence?"

"I—it's complicated, you know? The politics? The brass knows what they want to happen." He didn't know how much to say about the truth. He didn't know what to say about it.

"Hm." Jonas was quiet for a minute and sounded cautious when he finally spoke again. "They... wanted him?"

He should have known Jonas would catch on. The guy worked with all kinds of people doing all kinds of crazy shit.

"Yeah. Exactly. He was supposed to be the guy, no? Not me." But Sterling was, and no one could take that from him.

"So you're on their shit list, but you're going to ride anyway." To Jonas's credit, that wasn't really a question. "I get it, I guess, but you gotta have some balls."

"I'm a cowboy, not an athlete." And it was simple as that.

"Are you sure you're a cowboy? The porn cowboys leave their hats and boots on when they fuck." And there was Mr. Teeth again, grinning at him.

"Porn cowboys. Seriously? Those models with oiled chests? You are shooting low."

"Yeah, well. I know better now. You sure showed me how to shoot high, cowboy." Jonas snorted. "Pass me the bacon."

He handed a slice over and stole another fry. They were getting a little limp, but they were still perfectly edible. God knew he had eaten some crazy shit on the road.

"Okay, the bacon is cold." Jonas tossed it back on the plate. "I'm done." He got a quick kiss, and Jonas slid out of bed and started cleaning up and covering the leftovers, giving him a look at that pale little ass.

It was a great view, and it made him hum in

appreciation. His phone buzzed again, and Jonas looked up from rolling the food cart over to the door. "Whoever that is has been blowing up your phone for an hour."

He looked at his phone. "Yeah. I know." He'd been ignoring it, but now he was relaxing, he realized it might be home. He picked it up to see and found a line of texts from Chance, and he skimmed them. They said things like: *Where are you, Bit? Get back to me buddy, I'm worried now*, and *If Cody killed you, I'm going after his crew.*

The last one read, *You got one hour to get back to me and then I book me a flight to NY.*

Damn. *Sorry, man. I was in bed. Kicked Ball's ass last night.*

No shit? You're okay no?

All good. Better than. Hell, he was fucking fantastic.

Shit he deserved that. And you didn't even call me for bail or back up! Bobby's gonna love this.

I didn't. Not sure what he's up to today. Don't care. Sterling was busy with something far more fun.

Well good job. You off tonight? What have you got, two more days?

Jonas gave him a kiss on the cheek and mouthed "shower" at him before disappearing through their adjoining doors.

Coming home NYE I think. He guessed. He didn't care. Right now he had a hot son of a bitch in the bathroom.

Yeah, we're making some plans. It'll be good to see you. You seen the league website yet? You and Cody and those other aholes right there. What the hell are you wearing?

Fancy shirt. Jealous??

Right. Not a bit. You clean up good though.

Uh-huh. I'm a star huh?

Fuckin' A. Fancy. All the ladies will love you. He could just imagine Chance laughing at him.

Kiss my ass. Gotta go, man. Have a good one. He had to go. He wanted to see Jonas, slick and wet and pretty.

Sweet dreams, pretty boy.

He rolled his eyes and set his phone down.

The bathroom was full of steam, and Jonas was humming behind a thick, white hotel shower curtain. He could just see the top of the guy's head, fingers working shampoo into the dark wavy hair.

"You want company, honey?" *Can I look at you?*

Jonas chuckled. "I wouldn't mind."

"Good. I wouldn't either." Sterling slipped into the shower with Jonas. He didn't get to do this often—shower with another man, a man he'd slept with.

He felt Jonas's eyes take him in, slide over his skin like a touch. "Jesus. I'm trying to get clean, but you make me feel so dirty."

"Mmm." He watched the water slide down Jonas's belly. It was like a movie—slow and sensual, the steam making it a little fuzzy around the edges. Jonas caught him looking and grinned, making a show of rinsing the soap out of that thick hair, suds following a similar path. "Very nice. I should build a shower like this in my house."

He winked and dared to reach out, trace the line of water.

"Mm." Jonas watched him silently draw a line from sternum to hip, then leaned in for a kiss. Once their lips touched, Jonas turned them setting him up under the spray. "Everything okay at home?"

"Yeah. Chance was worried they'd taken me out and left me on the street, I think."

Jonas raised an eyebrow at him, and soapy fingers scrubbed at his head. "That was a possibility, I suppose."

"Yeah, I guess. Glad it didn't happen." That would have

sucked. He didn't know his ass from a hole in the ground in New York City, after all.

"Mm-hm." Jonas worked the shampoo into his hair and tilted his head back to rinse it out. "You've never been here before, right? You haven't seen the city at all, have you?"

"I haven't, no." He wanted to, though. Sterling wanted to go look at all the things, from Central Park to the Empire State Building to a good slice of pizza.

"You want to go out or stay in tonight? We could go see some lights if you want. And tomorrow your schedule is open until that PR party." Jonas scrubbed at his chest with a bar of soap.

"Wander around and look pretty, right?" He rolled his eyes. "Can we go see lights? Please? I'll send pictures home."

"Yeah. I'll totally take you around." Jonas's smile was genuine and adorable. "Rinse off, cowboy."

He stole a quick, wet kiss. "Sounds like one hell of a plan."

They finished up their shower and joked around while they got dressed, and by the time they left the hotel, they were both in a fine mood.

"I'm still so full. I may never eat again." Jonas turned his collar up against the cold night air and pulled a hat out of his pocket.

"Sí no, huh? I ate a week's worth." And he didn't regret it one bit. Well fed, well fucked—he was in great shape.

"We're in Midtown, so I think we should walk down to Rockefeller Center and see the tree, and you can see Saks all lit up. Grace will totally love that, you'll see." Jonas stayed close, in his space, close enough that they were constantly in contact as they walked.

"It's gorgeous, all lit up. Makes my luminarias seem

tame." Tame, but classy, and this was his first year in his own place.

"Luminarias?" Their hands brushed together, and Jonas's fingers tangled with his. Right there on the street. Holding hands. "Tell me about them."

"Oh, traditionally, you take a brown bag, put some sand in the bottom, and put a candle in. Now they have strung light ones and battery-operated candles." He pulled out his phone. "When we stop, I'll show you."

Jonas stopped them right there, smiling at him. "We're not in a hurry, are we? Let me see."

"Sure." He pulled up the photos. "These are at my folks'. They put up a load of them, huh? Line the house and the yard and the porch and everything."

Then he pulled up the pictures of his house.

His house wasn't quite as big, but it was nice, and with the luminarias, it was gorgeous. Classy. The flat roof was outlined with a simple string leading to the front door.

"Oh, how pretty. Is this your place? It's adorable." Jonas looked at it, smiling. "Really nice. I like it." Jonas took his hand again and tugged on him. "The tree is right around the corner."

"Yeah, I just had it built last year." They rounded the corner, and the biggest fucking Christmas tree on earth was there. "Whoa."

"I know, right? It's something. There's a big skating rink on the other side. I've never done the skating, but I like to walk by here around Christmastime, even with the crazy crowds. It's fun." They stood looking at the tree, and at the bright, lit-up, trumpeting angels that guided the way.

"That's cool. I do a lot of winter sport stuff but not ice skating. I have a couple of snowmobiles." God, that was beautiful. Seriously. So many lights.

He started taking pictures, unashamed of being the biggest tourist ever.

The clanging of a clock tower bell behind them made him jump, and Jonas turned him around.

"Oh! This is what I thought Grace would like to see. Saks. You watch, I'll get the video." Jonas pulled out his phone.

"Video?" Music started playing and the building lit up like a castle with chasing lights and colors, an incredible show. "Oh...."

He stood there, openmouthed and as tickled as a man with a feather up his ass. It was like Vegas, but Christmas.

"Amazing, right?" They had a pretty good view. The music and dancing lights went on for a while, and the show was impressive enough that they both stood there awed until the very end.

Jonas grinned at him. "I don't usually stop for this. I forgot how cool it is."

"Yeah. Yeah, man. That's... wow." Sterling couldn't stop grinning.

"Something good to remember about New York when you go home, instead of just cameras, blisters, nosy interviewers, and a fistfight." Jonas put an arm around his shoulders.

"Yeah. I'll have a couple other things to remember, man." One or two, at any rate.

"Maybe so." Jonas laughed.

They went around to the other side of the tree so he could see the ice rink better and all the skaters gliding and twirling. It was wall-to-wall people up there, though, so they didn't stay long. The crowds started thinning out a little as they made their way downtown. Jonas suggested they get a drink and was taking him to Times Square. "You watch the ball drop on TV ever? Or is that weird because it's not midnight in New Mexico?"

"They just show it two hours later. I always watch. It's... it's something you have to see, huh?" He couldn't imagine New Year's Eve without it.

"Well, I think so, but I'm from here. I didn't want to sound like I think everyone has to care what we do here in New York. I don't know how I'd say goodbye to the year without it. It's a ritual. A tradition." The street started getting brighter and brighter as they walked, lit up by electronic billboards and huge TV screens until the sidewalk was so bright it might as well have been daylight.

"Yeah, exactly. We usually have a little party and watch the ball drop. Do you come down here with all the people?"

Jonas laughed. "I did in college a couple of times. It's a crazy scene, getting here early, waiting around in the freezing cold. I'd much rather watch it at home or at a party with heat and elbow room."

"How early do you come?" He thought that it would be like bull riding in Brazil—wild and totally overwhelming.

"About noon if you want to be close and be able to see one of the stages. It gets crazy by about three. It's a long night. And you basically just don't drink anything because you don't want to have to pee. We're here." Jonas tugged him onto a pedestrian walkway that went right up the center.

"That's a long time to stand in the cold." He gawked and took pictures. "God, Grace is going to squeal."

Jonas squeezed his fingers and stepped close. "What about you, cowboy? Are you squealing?"

"Yeah. Yeah, I really am. This is like a movie."

"Good. You picked the best time of year to have to be in New York. I mean, it can get crowded, but it's beautiful."

"It's amazing." So different from his home, but so cool, so alive and sparkly.

"This year for New Year's I'm going to be packing for the beach and watching the ball drop from my bed." Jonas snorted. "Living on the wild side."

"Well, at least you have your vacation coming up, right?"

"A whole week at the beach. I had to cancel my last trip and I couldn't find a place there last minute, so I'm not sure where I'm going yet, but I'll figure it out. I don't even care where as long as it has a beach and someone to bring me a margarita."

"There you go. Texas has nice beaches. Cancun is cool. Nassau." He liked the ocean, but there was something weird about all that water.

"Any of those places would work. We'll see where I end up. You said your folks were going away next week? Will you watch the ball drop with Grace?"

"They're leaving sometime New Year's week, but I imagine I will."

"Did you get enough pictures?" Jonas took a step back and looked him over. "You interested in a drink? Or just another blow job?"

"I can't have both?" That didn't seem at all fair.

"Sure you can, just not at the same time." Jonas reached out and tugged him by his belt buckle. "I'll find us a pub. We have time to sleep in tomorrow, right?"

"Yes, sir." His cock reached up for Jonas's fingers, and he thumped himself. Damn.

They wandered through a big open area that was constantly changing color as the advertising on the billboards changed, past a giant set of red bleachers that were cool but seemed kind of randomly stuck there. Finally they turned down a side street and left the circus behind, then ducked under a kelly-green awning and into an Irish pub.

"I love these places, all the dark wood and everything."

The bartender waved them in. "Booth? Or there are two seats on the end there."

Jonas looked at him. "Your choice, cowboy."

"Booth, please." He wanted to see the city, but more than that, he wanted to learn about Jonas, about what he liked, about everything.

"Grab the one in the corner, guys. Lauren will be right over."

Jonas followed him over to the corner booth and slid into the seat across from him. "Good call. It's quieter over here." Jonas combed long fingers through dark hair, eyes bright. "What are we drinking?"

"I think I want a stout. You?" He could smell Jonas, smell the orange shampoo from the hotel, and it made him tingle.

"Hm. Something I can sip for a bit." One of Jonas's feet hooked around his calf. "Hmm. Black and tan, I think."

He shivered, goose bumps covering him. Damn.

They ordered their beer, and then Jonas leaned forward over the table and crooked a finger at him. "Come here."

He followed that finger like he was drawn closer. "You want something, honey?"

"Yeah." Jonas smiled and slid warm fingers along his jaw and then up behind his ear. "This."

He got a wink and Jonas produced a quarter, waving it in front of his eyes with a chuckle.

"Oh, very nice. I thought I washed behind my ears better than that." He rolled his eyes and laughed at himself for being a mooning calf.

"Aw." Jonas set the quarter down on the table between

them and took a quick kiss, smirking against his lips. "There. You looked so adorably disappointed."

"Well, how often do you get offered a kiss?" Not every day, for sure.

"Not nearly often enough." Jonas leaned back in his seat, watching him. "I wish you could have seen the look on your face watching that light show at Saks."

"It was so fucking beautiful, man. I can't imagine how long it took to set up." How many people and hours.

"Yeah. It was beautiful. The lights were impressive too." Jonas's eyes were on him, the expression so open he wasn't sure what it all meant.

Lord have mercy, the things Jonas made him want to do would frighten fish. "I want you, huh? All the way."

Jonas gave him a sweet smile, eyes searching his. "Me too."

Lauren, their server, set a bowl of pretzels on the table between them and set their glasses down. "Did you want anything to eat?"

Jonas shook his head. They were both still so full. "Not at the moment. Thank you."

"Okay, I'll check back in a bit." She hurried off again.

He lifted his glass with a smile. "Salud."

"Skoal." Jonas lifted his in a little salute and took a sip, then licked the foam off red lips. "Oh. Been a while since I had one of these."

"What is it?" He loved a good stout—it was like drinking bread.

"A black and tan? Well, it's Harp to about here." Jonas tapped the glass about halfway up. "And Guinness to the top. Strong flavor up front, lighter finish. Want to try it?" Jonas slid the glass across the table toward him.

"Lord yes. That sounds good." Sterling took a drink, humming over the flavor. "Huh. That's something else."

"I forget why I tried it the first time, but when I want something just to sip for a while, when I'm not in a hurry, I really like it. And I'm really not in a hurry. I'd like these next couple of days to last as long as possible." Jonas rested a hand over his.

"I hear that. Today's been...." He'd had a lot in twenty-four hours. Fighting, fucking, visiting. He wanted more.

"It's okay. I'm a little afraid to say it too." Jonas turned their hands over and smoothed a thumb across his palm, looking at it. "It's probably something that we shouldn't have let happen really, but it feels like it was meant to. I don't think I could have stopped it, it feels too good."

"We're both free and over twenty-one, man. I'm into you." He knew it was odd; he didn't care. Life gave no shits about what the world expected. You had to take what it offered.

Jonas took his beer back and winked at him. "I'm into you too. In case that wasn't obvious."

"I got the hint." He couldn't have fought his grin for love or money. "About round number four."

"Damn. It took you that long? I had you figured out after that howl in round two." His own grin turned into a laugh. Hell, they'd torn Sterling's hotel room apart.

"I'm slow on the uptake." He gave Jonas a wink. "But you got to admit I know how to ride."

Jonas's cheeks lit up pink, and the smile that went with it lit up those green eyes too. "Yeah. You're... you had me crazy. Stayed on a hell of a lot longer than eight seconds too. Impressive."

"Balance and core strength." He put his free arm up and swayed from side to side.

"Ooh. Sexy. I do like that core." Jonas laughed. "God. Could we sound any... hornier?" That last word just made the guy laugh harder.

"That's how you know that we got laid, honey. Otherwise we'd be too het up to play." That part he got, 100 percent.

"Het up. I like that. Like the hand jobs. You'd think I hadn't gotten off in... well. I guess it had been a while." Jonas snorted and sipped his beer. "My dad used to tell me if I felt like that, I should walk away, take a cold shower, and call on the girl another day."

"My daddy caught me with a cowboy named Jack in the barn when I was eighteen." No one ever stressed it. Except Jack had been pretty damn stressed.

"Oh shit. Was your dad cool about it? Was Jack?"

"My dad was pretty cool about the 'I like guys' part, less good about the 'humping a forty-year-old guy in the barn' part."

Jonas shook his head. "Yeah, well. The idea and the reality are different things for some people, I suppose. Although eighteen and forty? I mean, he might not have been real thrilled with a forty-year-old woman either."

"No. No, he wouldn't have. He has opinions about that. I was a desperate kid. I had no options."

Jonas snorted. "No, I guess you wouldn't. I got caught eventually too. Not at eighteen, though. I was a senior and I used a fake ID to get into a bar, and my dad had to come pick me up after the bartender took it away and called him. The car ride home was an experience, but mostly Dad was cool. And Mom didn't care about anything except that she didn't want me in a bar. Any bar."

"That doesn't sound too awful. I had a fake ID for the Burque, but it did me *no* good at home. Everybody knows my pop." He hadn't minded, though. They'd all known who to bribe to buy beer.

"Nah, it was okay in the end. I just really wanted into that bar, and after that, they knew me, so that didn't happen again. I had to find other ways to meet guys." Jonas grinned, flashing those teeth. "So I went to college."

"Ah. You went boy-hunting, did you?"

"Oh, don't tease." Jonas nudged him under the table. "You work in studly man central." Jonas winked at him. "Don't tell me that's not a perk. I've seen your ass in those Wranglers. You can't be the only one."

"Oh, Lord no. Not even close." He'd looked at way more than his share of Wrangler butts. "You just got to watch where your eyes fall."

Jonas put his beer down. "You mean watch who sees where your eyes fall? I heard Cody. It doesn't seem like it's a real accepting place."

"It depends. There's a lot of blustering. A whole lot of don't ask, don't tell. Some hand in the dark isn't cheating." There were a lot of land mines to avoid.

"I'd get myself in so much trouble. I'm just out everywhere now. I mean, I guess I could manage it if I had to, but it would feel... so strange."

Sterling understood that. It was hard to put the bull back in the chute once the gate was open. "It's not so bad at home, but working the league? You just have to know where you're safe."

"In my business nobody cares. You just need to get the job done. Actually in my business, clients don't care if you have a personal life at all most of the time." Jonas laughed. "And most of us don't have much of one. There's just no time."

He wasn't sure how that could be true. There was something about Jonas that drew his eye, constantly.

"It's a little hard to hang on to people. Friends and whatever. I miss things. I have to cancel last minute a lot. It frustrates my mother, especially around the holidays. But I love what I do."

"You can tell. Seriously. You take care of a lot of people."

"I do. Hopefully one day it will come in handy with people I actually care about. A husband, kids... a dog. I really want a dog." Jonas's eyes lit up. "A house... the whole thing."

"Yeah? I have a Saint Bernard. She's staying at my folks' right now." He'd never met a gay man who said he wanted kids. That was incredibly cool. A little unexpected, but cool.

"Really? A Saint? How neat. What's her name?"

"Lucy. She's amazing. A big, wonderful goofball." He pulled out his phone, found a picture of his dorky ball of fur.

Jonas took the phone right out of his fingers. "She is so cute! Oh, I love her. Wow. Beautiful." Jonas sighed and handed the phone back. "Yeah. I want a dog."

"She's a hoot. My folks have a pit, a coyote mix, and three cattle dogs. What kind do you want?" Somehow Sterling wanted to know everything—everything—about Jonas.

"I'm torn between an Aussie and a German Shepherd. Probably the Aussie. But they're both good with kids." Jonas tipped his beer back, nearly finishing it.

"They are. I've known some exceptional Aussies. Known some damn fine kids too." Things felt... heavy? Was that the word?

"One day, right?" Jonas leaned back in his seat, watching him. "I'll figure it out."

"I don't doubt you will. Me? I ride bulls until I cain't,

then I raise my bison." He pondered what all he was going to do in ten years, twenty, but the answers were all over the fucking place.

"I think I'm just going to focus on the next couple of days." Jonas hooked that foot around his calf again.

"I think you and I can fit in a lot of focusing. A lot." He winked, trying to ease the tension back down.

Jonas nodded, eyes locked on him, and he watched Jonas's chest rise and fall with a deep breath. "Yeah. I'm feeling pretty damn focused."

Christ, he couldn't stop smiling. "Well, then, Mister Burke, come show me what real focus is."

Jonas smiled back, left a twenty on the table, and slid out of the booth. "You're on, cowboy."

"Yessir. Let's go mess the bed up again."

11

J onas rolled over and tucked an arm around Sterling, breathing the cowboy in and holding on while he still could.

This time tomorrow Sterling would be finishing his last interview, taking his last few pictures, and that would be it. The cowboy would go back to New Mexico and the league and the things he loved.

And Jonas would be off for the beach.

But he couldn't help feeling like something was happening between them. It was undeniably real, and as impossible as it would be to follow through on any of it, he was feeling drawn to more than just Sterling's bed.

He'd known better. He'd known better than to go there, and he'd let it happen anyway. He and Sterling weren't fucking—they were making love. He wanted that connection and every one of those kisses, needed them like a drowning man needs air.

Time was against them, and that was just a fact he had to accept. His only plan for the day was to stay right here until the real world forced them out of bed. And they were getting close to that hour.

"Mmm... c'mere." Sterling dragged him in closer, still sound asleep. "So warm, babe."

"Yeah. You too." Jonas loved how they just fit together, how Sterling curled into him like he belonged there, all that lean muscle relaxed under his fingers. "I've got you."

"Got me." Sterling smiled for him, the expression so sweet it hurt.

They'd been in each other's arms since they left the bar the night before. Dozing between bouts of kisses, soft words, and more. He was sore everywhere in all the right ways, and the last thing he wanted to do was move. But that clock was ticking.

He watched Sterling's smile fade as the cowboy relaxed back into sleep and realized that thinking and worrying was no fun at all. They could rest up on their respective airplanes, right? He leaned in and kissed those sleepy lips lightly, intending to wake Sterling up as gently as possible, but wake him all the same.

"Mmm... morning, honey." Sterling nuzzled him, brushing their lips together.

"Late afternoon, more like." Could the man be any more beautiful? "Sorry to wake you. Only, not really."

"I don't mind. Waking up like this is magic." Sterling sounded like he meant it, all the way.

"It's like a dream." He kissed Sterling again, slow and light, just enjoying the moment, wanting it to last.

Sterling took one deep breath, then another, before stretching up tall, joints popping dramatically.

"You stretch like an old man." He grinned and blew a raspberry on Sterling's stomach.

"I been in a few wrecks in my time." Sterling cracked up, dragging him up for another kiss.

He took it, laughing as well. "Oh. I love this, but we have to get up, cowboy. You have to be all spiffy for the party tonight. We need showers."

"Mmm... no fair. Are you sure?" Sterling sighed dramatically, flopping into the pillows. "We could lie and say we went."

"Yeah. Let's do that. No one will miss you, right?" He rested his head on Sterling's chest and sighed, listening to the strong heartbeat.

"We'll just put a cardboard picture of me up there. No one will notice."

"That's a great idea. Then you can't say anything stupid." He lifted his head and grinned, showing off his pearly whites.

Sterling pinched him, and then the tickling started. "Stupid? Oh, you turkey buzzard."

"Ow! Fuck. Stop it!" Jesus, he was so fucking ticklish too. It was embarrassing. He wriggled and shoved at Sterling's hands, laughing, but the cowboy was so damn strong. "Dammit!"

"That's what you get." Sterling took a laughing kiss, bussing their lips together.

He hummed against Sterling. "No one has ever called me a turkey buzzard. I think maybe—"

His phone rang, the familiar opening to Beethoven's Fifth filling the room. "Shit. That's work." He rolled over and cleared his throat before he picked it up.

"Hey, Sid."

"Jonas. Everything good?"

Better than. "Great. What's up?"

"The league called. I wanted to give you a heads-up that

Cody Ball and some other guys are going to be at the party tonight."

Jesus fucking Christ. "Fantastic."

"Keep your cowboy clear, Jonas."

"On it." Like he had a snowball's chance in hell of stopping Sterling if the man wanted to start something. Or finish something.

"Have fun!" Sid hung up on him.

"Bastard."

"Everything okay?" Sterling had one hand on his belly, grounding him. He threaded their fingers together.

"Cody's going to be at the party." He sighed. "My boss says I'm supposed to keep you cool."

"Cool it is. I didn't start shit at the bar."

"I know. I'm not sighing at you, baby." He gave Sterling another kiss. "I don't like how ready they are to make whatever might go down your fault."

"You and me both, but I'll be on my best behavior. You have my word, huh?" Sterling was the one to sigh now. "You know, I was supposed to throw that ride, but I couldn't."

No, Jonas didn't think Sterling had it in him. He cared too much about things. Home, family. He was integrity in cowboy boots.

"What kind of a man would throw a ride? Cheat? I mean, who would you be if you had?"

"Not a cowboy, that's for sure. Now I just have to suck it up."

"Mmm." He winked. "Come on, maybe I'll suck it up for you in the shower." He slid out of bed before Sterling could stop him.

A pillow hit him right in the butt. "That was bad. Funny, but bad."

"It's gonna be good, though. Really good. You shouldn't

set me up for stupid one-liners." He ducked into the bathroom and started the shower, and by the time they got out, there was water everywhere and they were running late.

"Get dressed, cowboy. I'll tell them to go light on the makeup, hmm?"

"That would be a blessing, please."

He would do a lot for that smile. "I've got a car waiting. Be right back." He tightened the hotel robe around himself and hurried to his own room to get dressed. He didn't have time to think too hard about what he was wearing. He just pulled on his gray suit, a nice tie, and his good shoes, took a deep breath, and knocked on Sterling's door again.

"Come on in. I'm getting my boots." Sterling was in his jeans, an undershirt, and a black button-down, that hat right there on the bed.

"Oh, black. How very New York." And the man looked good in it too. "I went for the 'I'm working' look."

"Black shows blood less." Sterling got his boot on, then stood, looking him over as he opened his belt and started tucking in. "You look hot as hell, honey."

"Thank you. No blood, baby. Don't even joke." He blinked. "And I'd better not call you baby. Shit."

"No blood." Sterling stood there, watching him like... hell, he wasn't sure what that expression meant exactly, but it was blistering.

He stepped close, forgetting the time for a minute and offering a kiss. "It's the tie, right? Be good and I'll let you rumple my suit later."

"It's you." Sterling kissed him, hard enough that he thought it would be so easy to just call in stupid.

When Sterling let him breathe again, he took the cowboy by the shoulders and pushed him away to arm's length. "I wish.... We have to go. We'll be more than fashionably late soon." There wasn't time for wishing. He'd just have to catch his breath in the car.

"Right. No blood. No growling. No calling you anything too familiar. I'm on it."

Jonas laughed. "Save the growling for after." *Don't try to hold the cowboy's hand, don't stand too close, don't stare at him in that hot black shirt.* "Working. Got it."

He was so screwed.

"Working." Sterling popped that old hat on his head, the beads on the brim clacking together. "Let's hit it, darlin'."

12

L ord, there were a lot of people here pretending to be cowboys. The temptation to ask some random asshole in a goat-roper hat whether those shit-kickers had ever seen a cow patty was huge, but Sterling was working.

He wandered, staying near the wall, smiling and nodding on the way. He just needed to keep an eye out for Ball and his little minigang.

One of the cowboy wannabes headed his way, with a woman on his arm. She was in fringe and white boots. "Mister Kingsolver!" The guy stuck out his hand. "I'm Jim Davies. My company is one of the league sponsors."

"Mister Davies, pleased to meet you." He did meet and greets every goddamn weekend. This was just a big VIP box. "I hope you're enjoying this shindig."

"So far." Jim nodded. "I'm hoping for some dancing later. How is your win treating you?" The woman on Jim's arm was watching him, smiling.

"It's good to be the champ, hmm?" What was he supposed to say? Winning sucked? Because it didn't.

"Jim."

"Oh. I'm sorry, honey. Sterling, this is my girlfriend, Janie. Would you have time for a picture with her?"

Janie stepped closer to him like he'd already said yes. "How many girls can say they got a picture with a champion?"

"Well, obviously not enough." He grinned at her, nodded, and leaned in for the picture. "Everybody smile."

"Cheese!" Janie smiled for that picture, then stuck a hand into his back pocket and tucked herself right against him for another.

"Are you grabbing that cowboy's ass?" Jim laughed.

Janie giggled. "Would I do any such thing?"

"Hey, Sterling. I've been looking for you." Jonas swooped in like a pro, plucked Janie's hand right out of his pocket, and untangled them so smoothly that Janie seemed too stunned to protest. Jonas delivered her into Jim's arms and waved a hand at a waiter with a tray of glasses. "Are you two having a good time? Have some champagne on me."

"Yes. Well... thank you." The couple each took a glass, and Jonas steered Sterling away with a hand on his shoulder.

"Oh, you're good. I was feeling damn near violated."

"I'm in my element here, cowboy. I've got one eye on you at all times. Never fear. Are you having a good time?" Jonas straightened his collar and smoothed his shirt over his shoulders in a very professional way, though it was completely unnecessary.

"Honestly? Yeah. This isn't bad at all. Good music, friendly...." He stopped as he saw Ball and the others saunter in. "Here are our friends."

Jonas turned around and watched with him as the crew cut right into the center of the crowd, drawing attention and basking in it.

"No blood." It sounded kind of like Jonas was saying it out loud because they both needed to hear it. But then Jonas grinned. "Cody's nose looks a little rough, doesn't it?"

"Now that you mention it, he does look a little like he ran into someone's fist a couple times...." Didn't that make him smile?

"Imagine that." Jonas chuckled softly. "What do you want to do? We can give him a wide berth if you want, or—"

They'd been spotted.

"He's going to stay over there, right?"

"Just remember to stay back if they start throwing punches." There was no way Cody wasn't fixin' to try to get some of his own back. No way.

"Oh, shut up. I can throw one as well as I can take one." Jonas shook his head. "No. No one is throwing punches. Not here."

Sure enough, though, Cody made his way over, his band of assholes following close behind. The bull rider looked him up and down and then opened that trash mouth. "Well, if it isn't the champion himself, Sterling Kingsolver."

"Cody." That was all the bastard got. It was all he deserved.

"Are you enjoying the party, asshole?"

Sterling rolled his eyes, but kept his smile on. "I am. Lots of sponsors around, lots of folks to talk at."

"Good. I just came over to shake the hand of a dead man." Cody stuck his hand out, brazen as anything, plenty of people looking on. Sterling could feel Jonas suck in a breath beside him. "You do realize how hard it's going to be to stay alive when no one has your back, asshole? You won't make it one event before you're just a shitty, broke-dick has-been."

He figured he didn't have much choice but to shake that

hand because he'd promised Jonas he wouldn't throw the first punch, but he hadn't even stuck his hand out yet when another group of cowboys burst into the room, loud and happy, drawing everyone's attention, including Cody's.

Jonas's eyes went wide, but Sterling just took a quick breath. He'd know that wild laughter anywhere.

"Chance."

It was Chance—Chance and about twenty other cowboys, including the entire team of bullfighters, from head honcho Joe to Greg, who was so new Sterling didn't know the man's last name yet.

Cody looked stunned. "What the hell? Is that Joe?"

One of Cody's boys answered, "Yeah, man. And his whole crew, looks like. And Chance and Billy and Tom Little—"

"Shit. What is this about?"

"Chance?" Jonas looked at him and then back at the cowboys. "Is that your travel buddy?"

"Yessir. That most definitely is." And he was a lucky son of a bitch, wasn't he? "Hey, y'all! Way to make an entrance!"

"Hey, Bit!" Chance took his hand, bumped shoulders, and gave him a thump on the back. "We're maybe a little rowdy for this party, but we're just excited to be in the city."

"Hey." Joe stepped out of the group and offered a hand. "I don't think I got a chance to say congratulations in person, Bit."

Sterling stepped right up and took it, shook. "Thank you, sir. I appreciate it."

Cody stood there, watching with wide eyes, and Sterling began to wonder whether Cody really had the bullfighters in his pocket after all.

"Nobody ever figured you for a champ, but you rode like one the whole season. And you were a gentleman about it too. Took that title fair and square." One by one the members of Joe's team stepped up to shake his hand. They looked him in the eye, gave him nods, chucked him on the shoulder, told him congratulations.

Chance just stood to one side, arms crossed over his chest, staring Cody down.

Then Chris Martin—a three-million-dollar cowboy and one of the old guard—came up to him. "Hey, Bit, I want to introduce you to a couple three of my sponsors. They're gonna love you, and they're looking for cowboy blood."

Oh. Oh fuck. Fuck yes. Okay. Okay, you do this, Bit, you can put money away. Buy more bison. He stuck his hand right on out and gave Chris his number-one best smile. "That sounds like one hell of a deal. Lead the way."

Behind him, he heard Joe call Cody out. "You look like you ran into somebody's fist, man."

Jonas followed along but only until they were clear of the others, and then Sterling got a great big smile. "Just give me a wave if you need me. I'll have my eye on you."

"I'm counting on it." He couldn't stop grinning. "Stay close. I want to introduce you to Chance."

"Can't let you out of my sight, remember?" Jonas slipped away, leaving him to his business.

Chris introduced him around, and he smiled and chatted and let himself relax as more and more people seemed to respond. By the time he was done, he had shaken on three sponsor deals and had another in his pocket to think on.

Chris drew him aside, the famous cowboy staring into him with laser-sharp blue eyes. "Listen to me. Masterson ain't the whole league, no matter what he wants you to think. You're the champ. You rode the bulls, fair and square. You got friends here. Lots."

"Thank you, sir." He'd needed to hear that.

"Oh, I like these smiles!" Jonas came over, offering his hand to Chris, who shook it. "Mister Martin, very good to meet you. It's picture time, gentlemen. We have lots of candids, but we need a couple of formals. There are many more of you than we expected, a very nice surprise, so we're taking them in the foyer. Will you both come with me?"

Jonas led them out into the foyer, where the cowboys were being posed by photographers. "Sterling, we need you front and center."

"You got it." He dropped his voice to a bare whisper. "Anything you want."

Jonas blinked and cleared his throat, but recovered quickly. "Somebody let this troublemaker in."

The guys laughed and made room, dragging Sterling into the middle and gathering around him.

Cody wasn't nowhere to be found, Parrish either, but Travis McMartin was in the crowd. Made sense. The man had babies to feed.

These photographs were fun. The guys were posing and smiling, there was lots of laughter, and he didn't feel so much like the outsider he'd thought he was.

Jonas was watching him with a smile and the strangest expression. He thought maybe it was pride. And there was definitely heat in those eyes.

The photographer set them free, and he glanced at Jonas. How much more was there to do here? He wanted to talk to Chance, introduce him to Jonas.

"Hey, can we blow this Popsicle stand now?" Chance tugged his hat a little lower and looked around. "You're the celebrity. How does this work?"

Jonas headed right over. "You're done, Sterling. If you

want out, just make a show of it. Smile, wave, shake some hands while you head for the door."

"Good deal. Come on, y'all. Let's go." He headed for the door, trusting that Chance and Jonas would be there.

As he left, Cody Ball popped up like a bad penny. "You think you can get away with this, dickhead?"

He chuckled, nodded, and just gave Ball his best shit-eating grin. "Looks like I did. Have a good one."

"Later." Chance laughed behind him and followed him out.

Jonas headed for the curb and a black car waiting for them. He opened the back door. "Where to, Sterling? It's your night."

"Somewhere we can have a steak and a beer and hear each other talk, please."

Chance nodded. "A steak!"

"I know just the place. Slide in, guys." Jonas let them have the back seat and took the front with the driver, and Sterling realized the guy was still in work mode.

He slid in next to Chance, bumping their shoulders together. "Hey, buddy. How goes it?"

"Pretty damn fine, Bit. It's good to see you." Chance put an arm over his shoulders and squeezed.

"You... you brought all them? You shocked the shit out of me, swear to God." He couldn't be more pleased.

Chance grinned at him. "Well, it wasn't all me. Joe actually got wind of something Cody was up to, and I had heard the same something, if you know what I mean, and we put our heads together on it. I did suggest if Joe was coming, he should persuade them all to come, though. Cody needed that showing. You needed it too."

"I did. I got new sponsors, man. They were real positive." He couldn't believe it, but it had happened. It was a little like winning the championship, but better, because it was going to last longer.

"Good. That's what this party was for, right? Meet the sponsors, make some connections. I didn't know Chris was going to be there, but I do know he was impressed with you. He told me so himself the day after you walked away with your check. A handful of us figured out what was going down. Masterson didn't make much of a secret of it."

"Masterson is a league guy?" Jonas chimed in from the front seat.

"He cool, Bit?"

"Yessir. He's... more than." Sterling nodded to Jonas. "Masterson's a biggie wow. I didn't do what he said."

"Oh, right. He's the guy you told me about. I got it now."

"So what's your deal, you're like a handler? You have to follow him around?" Chance looked like he was sizing Jonas up.

Jonas nodded. "That's... pretty much it, yes. Follow Sterling around and make sure he doesn't get into trouble."

Chance snorted. "And you ain't fired yet?"

"I got close." Jonas started laughing pretty hard, and Chance jumped right in.

"Hey! I called in and apologized. Told them it was all my bad." He would suck it up for Jonas, and that was before any kissing.

"I appreciated that. I imagine that's the real reason I wasn't fired. But my boss was pretty ticked off."

The cab stopped, Jonas settled up, and they all stepped out onto the sidewalk. It was another cold night, and an icy wind was coming up the street. "Inside. Right there." Jonas pointed to a set of golden double doors set into a concrete facade.

"Man, this wind!" Chance was wide-eyed, one hand on his hat. "Lord have mercy."

Sterling cackled and grabbed the door, ushering them all in.

The place was way upscale, but they were treated like VIPs as they were shown to a table and handed enormous menus. This wasn't a place where you got a steak; it was a serious steakhouse.

Chance looked around like they was in a museum. "Would you look at this place?"

"They do a perfect porterhouse, of course," Jonas offered. "But their surf and turf is amazing, and they also have this coffee-rubbed New York strip. Oh my God. So good."

"Why would you rub a perfectly good piece of beef with coffee?" Chance looked at Jonas like he had two heads.

Jonas just laughed. "Don't knock it till you try it."

"You know what, I think I will." Sterling was feeling damn brave today, like maybe he could take on the world.

"Good for you." Jonas smiled at him, and the look made him wish for a second they were alone. "I'm thinking the strip and the lobster tail."

Chance put his menu down and leaned back in his chair, watching them. "So, when did y'all hook up?"

"What?" Did he just squeak? Seriously?

"You two. Bumping uglies. Cuándo?"

Jonas laughed and tried to play it off like the spin doctor he was. "Funny. Did you learn that one from Cody?"

"Oh, darlin', I've been bumping uglies a long time. My man is at the ranch waiting for me. You two look at each other like y'all can't not touch."

Jonas's eyes went wide. "Oh. Well. I knew that because Sterling told me about you, but I didn't know if he wanted...."

I thought we're working, and... uh." Jonas looked at him for help.

Sterling rolled his eyes, shaking his head at Chance. *Way to get my guy all het up.* "Couple of days. And he's hot as hell, and no, you don't get details. What steak are you ordering, man?"

"I thought I was helping. It's just the three if us, right?" Chance crossed his arms over his chest. "My apologies."

"It's all good. I was just.... I didn't know whether Sterling wanted you to know. But it's out there now, I guess so...." Jonas stood up, leaned over the table, and gave him a kiss. "I've been wanting to do that for hours."

Sterling sat there with his teeth in his mouth, just gaping. Well, he'd be goddamned. That was wonderful.

Jonas winked at him and then looked at Chance. "So... the rib eye?"

"Hell nah. I want the surf and turf. And chocolate cake."

Sterling glanced over. "In two days he's back on no carbs."

"Oh, like you." Jonas nodded and smiled at Chance. "Cool. Chow down, then. It's on the league."

The three of them ordered enough food for an army, and beer too, and laughed themselves all the way to dessert.

Jonas put his beer down. "I think the league is going to have to evolve a bit on what they want their cowboys to look like."

"What do you mean, like slick?" Chance tilted his head like a puppy that heard a whistle.

"Slick." Jonas laughed. "No, you misunderstand me. I mean that Sterling doesn't need to polish up to represent them well. Maybe it's better if guys don't. I'd rather see real cowboys, now that I understand what that is."

Chance leaned back in his chair. "Oh, Bit. I like him. I like him a lot. Keep talking."

Yeah. Sterling got that. He liked Jonas more than a lot.

"I was just thinking about how miserable Sterling was for that first interview. He was uncomfortable in the spotlight, uncomfortable in the stiff shirt and those godawful boots—they gave him horrible blisters—and... I mean, why be so miserable? If he'd been allowed to show up as himself, he'd have totally made those league guys proud. And remember I tried to make you change your hat? How stupid was that? Of course you should wear your own hat. God. So stupid. Someone should talk to them. Fix their marketing plan."

"I'll give Manny your number. He's always looking for ideas." Chance snorted. "And that's Bit's lucky hat band— his momma wove it, and Miss Gracie made the beads."

He'd told Jonas that very thing, but it meant something that his friend understood how important it was to him.

Jonas tilted his head. "Why does everyone call you Little Bit?"

"I started in junior rodeos, and I didn't grow until I was seventeen or so...."

"More like when he was twenty-one," Chance said.

"Shut up." Seventeen. Twenty-one. Who cared?

"So when are you going to get to a normal height?" Jonas flashed those goddamn white teeth at him.

"You thought I was plenty tall enough last night, honey." Oh, that was a good one.

"Mmm. True. You make up for it in muscle, anyway. I wish you could see your ass like I do."

Chance shook his head. "Wait... what's that? I think I hear my hotel room calling."

They all started cackling, drawing grins from the other

diners. About the time the laughter eased, one of them would start up and they'd be off again.

Jonas settled up with their server. "All right, it's bedtime for slightly drunk cowboys."

"I am not slightly drunk," Chance protested. "I'm mildly tipsy."

Sterling was just mostly horny, but that was something to whisper in Jonas's ear. So he just asked Chance, "What hotel are you in, buddy?"

"Same as you. We got us a group rate."

"That's cool. So is Cody, fair warning. Sterling's got one more interview in the morning, and then he's done. Are you guys on the same flight home?" Jonas's hand slipped into his as they stepped out into the cold air.

"I don't even know what airline you're on, Bit."

"Southwest."

"Ah. I'm on American."

Jonas gave his hand a squeeze and pointed up the street. "We can walk from here."

"We've got a little New Year's thing planned, Bit. Should be fairly family friendly. You could bring Grace if you want."

"Yeah? We'll see. Thanks." He didn't want to leave Jonas here. He wanted.... Hell, he didn't think he could have all that he wanted.

"I don't think I've ever been to a family friendly New Year's Eve party. Is there really such a thing?"

Chance laughed and winked at Jonas. "There's all kinds of family."

"Yeah. And Gracie is a killer card shark. She seems innocent, but she's wicked."

Chance laughed. "She's taken a few pennies off me, for sure. Is that the hotel? Already?"

"Yep. That's why I picked that steakhouse. Easy trip

home." Jonas's hand was hot in his, one thumb stroking the back of his hand.

He didn't intend to sit and bullshit with Chance. He had plans. Naked plans.

They stopped in the lobby near the elevators, and Jonas stuck a hand out. "It was really good to meet you, Chance. I can't believe what you did tonight for Sterling... all the guys and.... You're a real friend."

"It's the cowboy way. We have each other's back."

The words warmed Sterling through and through. That was it. The cowboy way.

"It's pretty amazing." Jonas turned those green eyes on him. "Ready to go upstairs, cowboy?"

"Yessir. Let's hasta." He barely touched Jonas's backside.

"Safe flight, Chance. It really was great to meet you." Jonas pulled him into the elevator.

"I'll holler." He waved and turned to steal a kiss as the doors closed.

Jonas opened for him, hands gripping his shoulders and pulling him close. He groaned and pushed closer, his eyes rolling with sheer pleasure. God, don't let the doors open.

As they crashed against the elevator wall, Jonas grabbed his ass and arched against him with a needy whimper.

"Yeah." He humped Jonas like a naughty puppy, totally unconcerned about when those doors might open.

"Fuck, Sterling. Need you." The doors did open, chiming cheerfully, and Jonas pushed at him. "Room. Naked."

"Yes, boss. I'm on it." He had that key card in his hand in a split second, and they stumbled inside as soon as he got it open.

"I saw it tonight." Jonas was breathless, tugging at his clothing. "The champion. The cowboy that beat everybody.

As soon as Chance and all those safety guys walked in, your eyes just... God. So hot."

He groaned and focused on working on opening Jonas's slacks. He needed skin. Their skin. Together. Now.

"Sit. Boots." Jonas shoved him onto the end of the bed and dropped to pull them off.

Damn, Jonas learned fast. As soon as the boots were off, he pulled Jonas up to fasten their lips together again. Jonas tugged and fumbled with his buckle impatiently, finally grunting out, "You do it," and going after his shirt buttons instead.

He managed to get them both naked from the waist down, while Jonas stripped away both offending shirts and one tie.

"Oh. Better." Jonas was on fire, hands all over him, lips locked with his except for a panting breath now and then.

Sterling was more than strong enough to take all that heat, all that need, and meet it with his own. This was going to be the best ride in recent history, and that was saying something.

Jonas broke off the kiss and dove across the bed for what was left of the strip of condoms he'd bought in the lobby shop a desperate night or two ago, and he grinned at how few were left.

"I'll call up for more." Sterling felt daring, amazing, and hot as all get-out.

Jonas tossed him one. "Your turn? Wait... where's the lube? Did it... is it on the floor?" Jonas flattened out and leaned over the edge of the bed.

"Uhn." He leaned down and licked a line up over one buttcheek before nibbling a little bit.

"Oh fuck. I... found it." Jonas moaned but didn't move.

"Mmm... good deal." He'd found it too. The perfect ass. So he licked again.

Jonas rolled under the touch, grinding into the sheets, pale ass lifting and lowering. "You make me insane, baby."

Oh Jesus, that was the finest sight ever, and he licked and nuzzled, his finger tapping that tiny, tight little hole.

He felt Jonas's shiver, watched that pale skin turn pinker, the blush rising everywhere. Finally, Jonas shifted and rolled under him, dragging him down into a kiss.

Sterling grunted as their cocks rocked together, lining up in the best possible way. *Oh damn, breathe.* No shooting over Jonas's belly.

"I want you. Please, Sterling." Jonas looked into his eyes, the look very like the one they'd exchanged across the bar at karaoke, but with... something more tender mixed in with the heat.

"You got me." And he meant that. Whatever Jonas needed.

"I need you inside me, Sterling. We can take it slow, I'd like to actually. I just... I need to feel you." Hot fingers slid over his skin like Jonas didn't think he was real.

"Need." It was the only word he could bite out, but he was busy covering his cock and not shooting his brains out of the end of his prick.

"Yeah." Jonas gave him a quick little show, slicking that hole with lube. "God, you look so beautiful."

He wanted.... Christ, he couldn't finish the thought. He'd never looked at a man and thought he could hold on forever.

Jonas held his arms open, inviting him, eyes watching him, body begging. "Come on, baby."

"Yeah, need you like breathing." He pushed up between

Jonas's legs, his entire body screaming to bury himself in his lover's heat.

"I know. God, I know. Kiss me." Jonas hooked his neck and pulled him down, meeting him halfway, teeth bruising into his lip. His cock nudged Jonas's hole and, when Jonas rolled his hips, he pressed in.

"Yes, yes. Fuck, baby." Jonas kissed him again, and he could feel his lover relax, the desperation becoming a slower heat.

"I got you." He began to move, nice and steady, filling Jonas inch by careful inch.

Jonas slowly arched under him, urging him deeper, lips parting and letting out a low, lovely moan. Sterling buzzed, riding the lazy need, the rhythm they found. Jonas wrapped around him, and Sterling swore he could feel them together everywhere.

"Perfect. So good." The words were whispered as Jonas lifted up, looking for a kiss. "Sweet. Just like that."

"Yeah, darlin'. Could do this forever." Forever. Oh man. What a thought?

"Gotta remember this one, right?" Jonas swallowed hard and moaned.

"Remember all of them." He intended to do this again, dammit.

Jonas held his eyes and nodded. "All of them, baby." His lover pulled him down into a kiss that seemed to be searching for his soul. He offered it up like it was his to give.

Lord forgive him, he must be in love.

Jonas's cry was muffled in their kiss and offered everything right back, ankles hooking across his ass and hot hands grabbing his thighs.

His balls began to tighten, and he pushed harder, freeing one hand to wrap around Jonas's needy cock.

"Oh God." His lover rolled, bucking up into his hand, ass going tight around his prick. "Please."

"Ask so pretty." His eyes crossed, that tight ring scraping along his shaft.

"You're just right, Sterling. Just... right. Fuck!" Jonas held on, hips rocking to meet his thrusts, working hard between his hand and his cock.

Sterling forced himself to focus, to watch Jonas because nothing had ever been so pretty.

Jonas let go of one leg, the freed hand grabbing the back of his neck so hard it made a slapping sound. "Sterling!" His lover arched, using that grip as leverage, and Jonas shot hard, head snapping back and hips grinding against him.

"Love." He groaned softly, one hand still drawing out Jonas's pleasure. His own need was right there, and he gritted his teeth, the world going fuzzy as he came.

"Love. Yes." Jonas was still raking in breath but kissed him anyway in the short spaces between.

Oh fuck yes.

"Stay for New Year's, go home after. Don't leave tomorrow. Don't."

"I won't. I'll stay." He could call home. Apologize. Gracie would understand.

"Good. Okay." He could feel Jonas relax a little, the tension in his lover's face smoothing out into a smile. "Yeah, good. Better. Thank you."

"So good." He rubbed their noses together, laughter bubbling up inside him. "Whoa, honey."

"Better every damn time." Jonas played at nipping his nose, grin growing wide. "You're a little wild, cowboy. I was totally gone."

"Yee-haw." It was the hottest friggin' thing ever, no question.

Jonas started to giggle, trying at first to keep it in, but it wasn't working, finally bursting into full-out laughter instead. Sterling snorted, chuckling against Jonas's throat, the sound crazy muffled.

"Turd." Jonas sighed and slid a hand over his back. "Sterling."

"Yeah, honey." He inhaled and breathed Jonas in.

"I think...." Jonas's fingers dug into his ass. "It's gonna be a long night."

13

Jonas watched Sterling smile, shake hands, and be the charming cowboy he was. The interview had been the best one yet, and the shoot was going well. Jonas hadn't insisted Sterling dress at all, or spend too long in makeup, and Sterling seemed much more relaxed, much more himself. That made the cowboy that much more at ease in front of the cameras, and that much more handsome.

Handsome, sweet, funny, talented, hot as hell, and man, Jonas wanted that cowboy. Every bit. But he couldn't tether someone like Sterling to New York forever. Jesus, he no idea what he thought he was doing.

He had asked Sterling to stay, but now he felt like all he'd done was put off the inevitable for another couple of days. Part of him regretted setting himself up to go through that all over again.

"Let's have a laugh, Sterling. A great, big...." Sterling's laughter echoed in the small studio, filling everyone with joy and making them smile. "Perfect!"

Perfect. Fuck. What was he going to do?

As soon as Sterling was done, those eyes were fastened on him, warm and happy and not worried at all. How could Sterling not be worried?

"You looked just like a star up there, Sterling. I think you're getting the hang of this." He smiled, letting Sterling's confidence work for him too.

"I just got to be comfortable. That's easy enough, huh?" Sterling leaned so close Jonas could feel his body heat. "I want to kiss you, honey. So bad."

He felt himself flush, the warmth spreading all the way to his toes. Yeah, that's what he wanted too. He swallowed hard and took a step back. "You better go get your makeup off, Romeo."

Moments like this one made him want to rationalize everything between them as just sex, and he'd try to convince himself that was all it was. But then Sterling would smile, exactly like the cowboy was doing right now, and Jonas had to admit he knew better. He wanted more.

"Yeah, this stuff is heavy and sticky, huh? Time for a wet paper towel." Sterling's hand was warm where it brushed across his belly.

He caught Sterling's hand quickly and gave it a squeeze. "Think about what you want to do for lunch." He needed to stay out of the hotel room, just for a little while, just to make sure his head was clear, because this was crazy. Everyone was going to think he was insane. And then there was Sid, who was going to give him the big, fat "I told you so" when Sterling went home and he was back in the office trying not to mope. He couldn't count how many times he'd heard Sid give the seduction speech. "Don't get drawn in. They're using you."

Except Sterling absolutely wasn't.

He sighed. Sid would raise an eyebrow at that statement too.

So what was this going to be? A long-distance thing? Sterling might have won some money, but neither of them had the cash to fly back and forth across the country. FaceTime sex? God, that sounded depressing and... unsexy.

What the hell were they supposed to do about this? He wanted to call it a fling, a wonderful little affair, but part of him knew better.

Fuck it, he had a hot cowboy to play with. He should shut up and enjoy the man. He knew damn well it wasn't real anyway. They were from two different worlds. It couldn't possibly work. He needed to tell his infatuated heart to back down.

Right. That was it. He had to be practical, so he'd enjoy the cowboy while he could. Period. He waited by the elevators for Sterling to get back, looking out a window over busy Midtown. He'd never seen it more crowded than when New Year's Eve was on a weekend.

"Hey, honey. I'm back to normal." Sterling touched the back of his hand.

"Hey." His skin lit up, just that little touch enough to make him shiver, and he tangled their fingers. He just had to hope no one professional was watching. "Did you decide on food?"

"Take me somewhere you love?" God, Sterling wasn't going to let him be distant.

He could maybe play like he didn't get it. He punched the elevator button. "I could go for a burger."

"Okay. You know I'm pro-meat." Sterling bumped shoulders with him, offering him one of those warm, happy grins.

He hadn't ever seen anything more beautiful. How could he not enjoy that? How was he going to let that go?

They got on the elevator, and as the doors closed he let himself smile back. Two more days. Why ruin them with worry? "I'm pro-fries. Maybe sweet potato ones."

"Oh, I am a cowboy. Until the first, all fried foods are my friends."

He leaned close, giving in. "You should kiss me before the doors open."

"I can most certainly do that." Sterling grabbed him up close, smiling into his eyes. "God, you're fine to me."

Then Sterling kissed him like he was the most necessary man on earth.

He knew just how his lover felt, because he felt himself just open up and give it right back. He needed this. Fuck, he needed Sterling.

He was so fucking screwed.

The elevator doors opened, and he tore himself away. "So... burgers."

"Uh-huh." Sterling blinked at him as if he was dazed, swaying. "Burgers."

That was his fault. He did that to Sterling. God, he felt fifteen feet tall. "Come on." He took Sterling's hand and led him out to the sidewalk, deciding not to care right now who saw them.

Sterling laughed and followed along, nudging him whenever they got close enough. "Everyone's so excited, huh?"

"Yeah, when the ball drop is on a weekend, the party starts early." It was freezing out. Downright frosty, the wind finding its way down his back despite his scarf, but the streets were busy. Midtown was already lit up bright like it was the middle of summer, and it wasn't even dark yet.

"Right. Are we going to stay at the hotel tonight?" Sterling blew out a breath. "It's snowing back home."

"Is it? Uh. Shit. Well, we can, but it's pricey, and you're off the clock. I sure can't afford it."

"Would you show me your place?" The request was gentle, quiet, almost tentative.

Fuck. Sterling in his apartment? In... in his bed? There was no undoing that, was there? But he saw what was in Sterling's eyes, and he knew what it would do to his lover, and to them, if he said no. He nodded. "Sure. Let's go pack up."

"Sounds amazing, honey. I can't wait to see."

"Don't get too excited. You'll be disappointed." He turned the corner and tugged Sterling into the hotel.

Someone had already come by and removed the wardrobe rack, and they checked out barely half an hour later. He dragged Sterling down into the subway since the cars weren't being paid for anymore.

He was nervous. His place was neat and clean—he was a neurotic about that—but it was small. Really, really small.

Good thing Sterling was small too.

Sterling was taking everything in, the smile on his face wide and eager.

Once they were settled on the standing-room-only train, he grinned at Sterling. "First subway ride?" He was glad it wasn't July. No one should get their first whiff of a subway, or its riders, in July.

"Yeah. Pretty damn cool, huh?" Sterling beamed at him, eyes lit from within.

"It is." He looked at his cowboy—*his cowboy*. Wow. "So do you like the city?"

"I do. It's so different, so alive."

"Right? It has its own pulse." He nodded, watching

Sterling and wishing he knew what it would take to convince a cowboy to stay in the city.

"I like that. It does feel like that, doesn't it? Where I'm from does too. It's just way older."

Yeah. That was what he thought. Never happen.

Their stop came along soon enough, and he made his way up to the street through a maze of tunnels without thinking. He could find his way home in his sleep. "We can drop our stuff off, and then the burger place is just a couple of blocks walk."

"Sure. I can't wait to see." Sterling shot him a worried smile. "Thank you for letting me come over."

Jonas leaned in to drop a quick peck on Sterling's cheek, then gave him a nod. "You're welcome. I mean that. Come on." He turned down a street very much in shadow at this time of day and stopped at the first set of steps. "Take a deep breath. It's a lot of stairs."

"Good to know. What floor are you on?"

"Five." He started the schlep up. He was used to it by now and could do it with groceries or furniture. He could even do it dead drunk. But he liked it because the top floor got all the light. The lower floors had no view and were in shade of other buildings almost all day. He headed down the hall to the door at the very end and took a deep breath. "This is me." *This is embarrassing.*

"Man, no wonder you have thighs like rocks. I bet you could ski like a master." Sterling didn't look so worried anymore.

"I can ski. I haven't in a while, but I can." *Thighs like rocks. Ha.* "Come on in."

He held the door and let Sterling into his tiny main room area first, glancing quickly at the bed to make sure he'd made it. He pointed. "This is the living room, bedroom, and office. That's the kitchen, and the bathroom is the door next to the fridge."

But his was the unit at the very front of the building, and the main room had three windows along the one wall.

"Very cool. Lots of light." Sterling headed over to the windows and peered out.

He watched Sterling and smiled, carrying his things into the room and setting them down on the bed. Maybe two grand a month for a hole-in-the-wall was more impressive than it seemed. "There's a chair there you can put your bag on."

"Thank you." Sterling looked at him before stepping right into his space. "You look unhappy, honey. You okay?"

He waved it off, not wanting to get into anything. He slid his arms around the cowboy's waist. "How could I be unhappy with you standing right here?"

"Oh, that was smooth. I like it." Sterling took his hat off, set it aside. "Kiss me, huh?"

"Yeah." He touched his lips to Sterling's, and the doubt melted away. He opened up for his lover and curled his fingers around Sterling's shoulders. Damn, Sterling kissed him like they were starving and nothing on earth was better.

"Jesus, Sterling," he whispered. "Every time we kiss I feel like nothing else matters."

"That's because it doesn't. This matters. We matter."

"We matter. Sterling, we have two days and then—" *No. Don't go there. Don't do that.* "Never mind. I don't want to talk about it." He kissed Sterling again to stop the conversation.

Sterling watched him, even as they kissed, eyes searching his face.

He pulled away with a sigh. "Don't look at me like that. Let's go get burgers."

"Like what, honey? I just want to see your life and then take you home to see mine too."

"You pretty much lived my life for a week. I'm only here when I don't have to be somewhere with someone else." He ignored Sterling's talk about visiting. "It's not boring, but it's not... I don't have a lot of life that's not centered around work. I don't have time usually."

"I understand—I have on-the-road life and ranch life. Sometimes I feel caught up."

He nodded. Well, that was interesting. With Sterling on the road, it would have been a long-distance thing no matter what, wouldn't it? Even if they lived together, they wouldn't have been together half the year or more.

"Life is crazy sometimes." Jonas shrugged.

"Life is always crazy, but that's okay."

He smiled. Maybe it was, maybe it wasn't. But he had Sterling to himself right now. "Okay, you want to see how I live? I'll give you the grand tour." He stepped away, gesturing like a tour guide. "On your left we have the living room, anchored by a cleverly cockeyed couch and my grandfather's Army trunk, which makes an excellent coffee table and doubles as my linen closet."

He winked at Sterling. "Turn just slightly to your right, if you would... good, just like that. In front of you is the bedroom, where precious little shenanigans have taken place in the last few weeks, so you are a very welcome guest."

"Mmm... shenanigans. I would like to shenan with you, eh?"

"Bring it on, cowboy. We can shenan-again anytime you're... up for it." He winked and gestured to the kitchen. "Not much goes on in there either. I have cereal and cans of soup, and I think maybe there's ice cream in the freezer."

"My kitchen is never like that because of Momma. She put in a deep freezer for green chile, and she uses my fridge as a second when I'm not home. I like cooking, though, outside mainly. We got a huge deal outside for the families."

"The families? Plural?"

"Well, I got a shit-ton of cousins, their kids. They live all over northern New Mexico and southern Colorado. My Uncle Ernesto has a place in Durango. It's a bit of a drive, but we get together for holidays and all."

Jonas missed his family. They were everywhere now. But they all visited the city every couple of years, so he got to say hello. Instagram and group texting was his friend.

"That's really cool. I'd love to meet them all someday. See who you come from." He most wanted to meet Grace and Sterling's parents. He loved how Sterling talked about them, cared about them.

"So come home with me. I'd love to show you my place. It's not a beach, but there's mountains and all. Good company, good food, a fireplace, and a big ole bed...."

This was starting to physically hurt. His stomach seized and his heart ached. "Sounds great, but... we can't do that." He gave the cowboy a half smile and shrugged.

Sterling blinked, giving him a confused look that broke his heart. "Why on earth not? My people would love to meet you."

"That's sweet." He didn't understand how Sterling could talk that way. He stepped away and opened his suitcase, pulled out jeans and a sweater. The apartment was starting to feel even smaller than it already was, and he wanted out of his tie before they went out. "What do you want to do tonight?"

"I'm easy. Whatever makes you happy, huh?"

"More karaoke? Dancing?" He stripped off his tie and

dress shirt and pulled on a T-shirt and a light sweater. Whatever they did he wanted it to be fun, and he wanted to end up back here wrecking his bed. Tomorrow he'd take Sterling for brunch, and then they'd hide from the crowds and craziness at home, watching it all on TV.

"Do you like to dance? I haven't been in a long time." Sterling watched him closely, like he was about to bolt.

He had no idea how to handle Sterling right now, so he just wasn't going to. "I do. I go when I can. I don't love it when my clients want to go because they're easy to lose in a club, but I dance." He tossed his shirt in the hamper and his pants in his dry-cleaning bag and pulled on his jeans.

"I'm not your client anymore, so that's okay." Sterling came up to him, hugged him tight. "Do you want me to get us a hotel room? I didn't mean to make you uncomfortable, honey. I just wanted to see where you hang your hat is all."

"No." That was an easy answer. Why it was easy was the complicated part. He put his arms around Sterling and returned the hug. "You feel good. I'm.... Being here isn't making me uncomfortable. I was nervous about you coming here because it's small and not at all what you're used to, I'm sure, with all those acres and everything."

"Bah. I been in rooms all over. I lived in a tiny house for a while even that made this apartment look like a mansion. I sleep in my truck a lot to save money."

He stood there in Sterling's arms, willing his worry away, not at all ready to let go. "Boilermaker down on First has great burgers. Actually their fries are even better."

"Cool. I like both burgers and fries." Despite the words, Sterling held on.

"I could stay like this forever." He sighed. "We better get some food, though, before we're both hangry." Maybe they could just order in.

"Let's get delivery. I want to hold you, honey. We can dance here, even."

He nodded. "I'd love that." He finally slipped away from Sterling and pulled out his iPad so they could look at menus. "So are you glad you're done with this round of shoots? Have they lined you up for anything else?"

"The season starts in three weeks. It's crazy, because there's stuff in every city."

"You're competing and you have shoots in every city too? Jesus. That does sound crazy." See? Never home. Even if he did visit the cowboy in New Mexico, Sterling was going to be on the road after that.

"Yeah. Chance says we need someone like you to help out, now that the league is getting big."

"Probably a good idea. I'm sure they'll find the right cowboy for the job. How do you like your burger?"

"Pink." Sterling moved back to stare out the windows again.

"Pink. Got it." He ordered two burgers and curly fries, watching Sterling's back as he went to the fridge for a couple of beers. He might not have much food, but he always had beer. Always.

He opened them both and joined Sterling at the window. "Kind of a classic New York apartment view." He set a beer down on the window sill for Sterling.

"It's neat. So different. I miss my sky, though. I want to show you. It goes on and on." Sterling cackled suddenly. "Unless it's snowing. That's gray."

He rested a hand on Sterling's back. "That's gray here too." He sipped his beer, thoughtfully.

"Yeah. You think that could happen? Snowing in the sunshine?"

"Maybe? I've seen it rain that way. My grandmother used

to call it liquid sunshine." He rubbed a hand up Sterling's spine. "It was one of her favorite things."

"My granny said that meant it was going to rain tomorrow at exactly the same time. She was always wrong."

He dropped his forehead on Sterling's shoulder and sighed. Sterling was right—things had gotten uncomfortable between them, and he didn't want that. "It's not that I don't want to see your place, or meet your family."

"What is it, then?" Sterling reached back for him, hand solid and warm.

"Honestly? Sterling, even if I did come visit next week, what happens after that? Where are we say, in a month? I mean, how do you see this working?"

"I don't know! We'll just have to see what happens. Can't we do this? Just try?"

"I don't know." He sighed and sat down on the end of his bed. "What's the best-case scenario here? When would I see you again?" Assuming he could get time off whenever that was.

"I ride on the weekends. I'll try to come out here before my first ride, if you want. I can afford that."

"If I don't have to work, I would like that." Sterling had a million-dollar purse in the bank. The cowboy was in a better position to buy a plane ticket than he was. "And if we're going to try this, I'll come visit this week instead of going to the beach." That was only fair, if Sterling was going to make an effort too.

This all seemed so complicated, but if Sterling really thought they should try... what was he going to say? No?

"Do you want to give up your beach?"

"Well, this is how it works, Sterling. We're going to have to make some compromises. I don't guess you could come with me and go home after?"

"Let me check when my people are leaving. I can't leave Gracie in the lurch."

"Sure. Yeah." Jonas knew Sterling had promised to spend some time with her while his folks took a vacation. "If not I'll come back with you."

"Okay." Sterling sat too, staring out the window. "I feel like I ought to apologize to you."

"What? Why?" He leaned closer, watching Sterling.

"I don't know, honey. You seem so damn sad."

He slid a hand into Sterling's. "I'm worried. I'm going to miss you. The one time I tried the distance thing it... it turned out to be too hard, and we broke up on the phone from three thousand miles away. It sucked."

"I know we've only just met, but I'm not the fuck-you-over kind."

"You? I never thought...." He sighed. "Technically I fucked him over. But it hadn't been working for a while. It's hard, Sterling."

"I'm sorry. Really, honey. I don't want to be the guy that makes you sad."

He nodded. "I don't want to be the guy that lets you down. You deserve better than that."

Sterling squeezed his hand and sighed. "Tell me what you want to do tomorrow?"

He took a big breath and found a smile for Sterling. "I am going to take you to brunch, where we'll stuff ourselves silly. Then we'll drop by the grocery store and pick up stuff for dinner and snacks to keep us happy here until the ball drops, because we don't want to be out there dealing with craziness, right?"

"Right. I'm all about avoiding the crazy."

Yeah, Jonas believed that. Sterling was a rodeo cowboy. Crazy was what he was. He didn't believe for a second that having a relationship with Sterling wasn't all about the crazy. Or just plain insane.

"Got enough of that without drunken New Yorkers." He shifted to look at his lover. "Listen. Regardless of how all this works out, we have well over twenty-four hours of time together. I'm not planning on being a bummer for all of it." He kissed Sterling and smiled. "So, what's your favorite guilty pleasure movie?"

"*The Day After Tomorrow*."

He raised an eyebrow, smirking. "So... that's for real? Or is that a metaphor?"

"Yeah. You know the disaster movie? I love it. It cracks my ass up."

He laughed. He should have known—Sterling was too kind to make that type of joke. "I know the movie, yes. It will go perfectly with our burgers."

Sterling beamed at him, then leaned forward for a kiss. The buss was gentle, but it lingered. "Sounds like a great day."

The doorbell rang, making them both jump, which then made them both laugh. Jonas hopped up to get the burgers. "I'll be right back. Grab the remote and find your movie." He hurried down the steps to the door building entrance, but moved considerably more slowly on the way back up with the food. "God, it's so cold out there."

"Right? It's snowing hard back home, but it's not so cold." Sterling took the food from him. "That smells delicious. Honest."

"This place is awesome. You're going to love it. I wish we'd gotten snow like they said we might. The city is pretty when it's snowing. Did you find the movie?" He was unpacking food while he babbled at Sterling, his stomach growling. God, he didn't want to do this. Finishing this meal meant one less meal with Sterling.

"I did. Netflix. You have a great setup here. You want anything besides your beer?"

"Nah, I'm good with the beer. You?" He set their spread out on his trunk with a roll of paper towels, loving the grin he got for his trouble.

"I'm golden. God, this looks amazing. I love a good burger." Sterling nudged him. "I want to take you to Blake's for a green chile cheeseburger."

"Ooh. Do they put the chile in the burger or on top?" He took a huge bite, mostly because there was no such thing as a small one with these burgers. "Mmm."

"On top. It's the best. Seriously. The best."

He picked up the clicker and hit Play, then pointed to his burger and gave Sterling a thumbs-up. That was the best he could do. He wasn't going to pull out his toothy grin with his mouth full.

Sterling devoured his burger. Seriously, the man had to have a hollow leg. There was no way all that food could fit in that little body.

He picked up a french fry and held it in front of Sterling's eyes. "You have room for this too?"

Sterling opened up and ate the fry with a snap.

He laughed and leaned close. "How do you not get sick eating that fast?"

"I've spent a lot of meals standing up and powering through. If I had a dime for every Navajo taco...."

"You'd open up a taco joint?" Man, he'd do a lot to stay close to that smile. He'd never know another one like it.

"I'd have enough cash for a storefront and two taco trucks." Sterling winked over. "What's your position on Navajo fry bread?"

"On what?" He laughed. "My position is clueless. I've never eaten anything with the word *Navajo* in front of it."

"No shit? I'll have to make sure you get some. It's good stuff."

"I've never been out there. I was in San Francisco for a few days on vacation once, and I spent a long weekend in Vegas, but I didn't get the chance to travel around." He shifted on the couch and threw a leg over Sterling, sitting on his lover's knees. "So if the beach can't happen, you can show me around."

"I've been all over. That's the best part of the job—going and doing." Sterling reached for him, petting him in long, slow strokes.

"How about the staying and doing? You like that part too?" He bent down and touched his lips to Sterling's, feeling a little buzz building and wanting to ride it out for a while.

"I love to be home. I haven't been in my place long enough for it not to be new."

He chuckled softly, taking another gentle kiss. "I meant me, cowboy. Staying and doing... me."

"Oh, honey." Sterling beamed at him, one hand sliding up his thigh. "That's heaven on earth."

"Yeah." His eyes locked with Sterling's, and their rich darkness seemed to be begging him to say what was really on his mind. "Hey." He drew a finger along his lover's jaw. "Sterling, I—"

He sighed, startled by his cell phone ringing. He started to ignore it and smiled at Sterling, but he knew it was fucking work and ignoring it would just mean a phone call later. They'd already been interrupted.

"I'm sorry. Don't move." He winked and dragged his phone off the kitchen counter. Which was barely arm's length from the back of his couch. Crap, it really was Sid. "Hello?"

"Hey, man. Lulu is in town, and she needs you."

What the hell did that mean?

"Mia's got her covered, Sid. Remember? I'm—" Shit. No, he wasn't working. Did Sid even know Sterling was still in town? His boss certainly didn't know Sterling was sitting on his couch. "I'm busy. On vacation. I'm not working."

"Yeah. I'm sorry, Jonas. Mia got a big gig, and she can't cover."

"Well, then, I'll see Lulu on Monday, okay? I can't this weekend." He'd give up his vacation if he had to. Just put it off again and go see Sterling in New Mexico later.

"Jonas, I wouldn't ask if it wasn't important."

The thing was, it wasn't a question. There was no doubt that he had to do this. He looked at Sterling, not sure what he was seeing in his lover's expression.

"Sunday?" He knew damn well that wasn't going to fly. "Lulu needs you" meant a hell of a lot sooner than Sunday. But he needed to try. He and Sterling had plans. He'd asked the cowboy to stay in the city with him. He already felt the dread creeping up his spine.

"She's got a party at ten. She'd like you to be there."

"Tonight?"

"I'll text you the address and your hotel info. You'll need a suit tonight. She also suggested you bring a bathing suit."

Jesus, Lulu. "All right."

"Hopefully you'll get your vacation in a couple of weeks. The beach isn't going anywhere."

A couple of *weeks*?

"Jonas? You there?"

He sighed. He couldn't even look at Sterling. "Yeah. Yeah, I'm here. Tell Lulu I'll be there."

He ended the call and looked at his phone as he sank back into the couch, knowing Sid would be texting him any second with details.

"That was work." Like Sterling wouldn't have figured that out for himself already. The text came through; he'd be staying at a pricey Midtown hotel. "Dammit."

"Are you going to get to finish your burger?" Sterling gave him a wink, a nod.

He snorted. "Yeah. I have a couple of hours. I'll need a shower, though, and I have to iron a shirt. I should probably figure out what's clean in my suitcase. I have to call Lulu a car. And I guess I better check into the hotel before this party—" He looked at Sterling. "I don't guess you want to share my hotel room?" Jesus, he could feel his work-brain kicking in already.

"Would that get you in trouble with your boss?"

"Better to beg forgiveness than ask permission. I mean Sid ruined our night, so I'm not sure I care what the rules are." Well, this was interesting. He'd been inconvenienced, he'd been annoyed before, once or twice he'd been kind of ticked off, but he'd never been upset. He'd never felt angry about being called in to work. It was just how work was. But today was different.

"Okay, then. Let's do it."

Sterling surprised the hell out of him.

"Yeah? I still have to work, but at least you'll be there after the party, and while you're waiting for me, you can relax in style." Hell, he'd even consider bringing Sterling to the damn party too.

"Works for me, honey." Sterling bumped shoulders with him. "Finish your burger."

"Right, okay. And then a shower." He only had a few bites left anyway, and he inhaled them like he hadn't eaten in days. He wanted to stay in the moment with Sterling, but he was gearing up to work now, going through his checklist in his head, reminding himself what Lulu would be looking for, thinking of things he needed to find out about this party.

14

J onas watched Lulu schmoozing at the bar, and covered up a yawn. An hour ago he thought for sure this party was wrapping up, but then Lulu got to talking with a couple at the bar, and they bought her a drink. Now, two more cosmos later, the bartender had become her best friend, and Jonas was beginning to realize he wasn't going anywhere anytime soon.

The clock on the wall above the bar said 2:00 a.m. How many years had he been doing this damn job? He ought to have known this was how it was going to go.

He pulled out his phone and started to text Sterling for the third time in the last hour, but he had no idea what to say. He knew the cowboy understood that work was work, but he'd told the man he'd be done soon twice already.

He knew that the moment he let Lulu out of this sight, she'd be looking for him again, but he had to call this time, talk to Sterling, and just be honest. He had no idea when or if he'd be back to the hotel tonight.

The phone rang twice as he ducked out into the hallway

where it was quieter, and he wondered if Sterling had fallen asleep waiting for him.

"Hey, honey. How goes?" Sterling sounded tired, but not angry.

"Hi, you. Did I wake you up?" That was probably a stupid question.

"No, sir. I'm watching movies. How's your party going?"

It wasn't his damn party. He didn't even want to be at it. He wanted to be home in bed with his cowboy. "I've had better nights." He leaned against the wall and sighed. "I'm... I don't have any idea if I'll be back tonight. I'm really sorry."

And I miss you.

"Long party, huh?" Sterling sighed. "That so sucks. You got you a cup of coffee?"

"I've had two, and I'm yawning anyway. Is it a nice hotel? Did you get room service?"

"It's fancy, huh? I wasn't hungry, but I ran downstairs and grabbed me a Coke and a candy bar."

"Lulu always picks fancy places. You should eat. It's on her. Or maybe have a beer or something." He couldn't talk long. He was going to have to hang up and get back to the party before Lulu missed him.

"Maybe I will. I'm pretty comfy right now. You think you're going to be getting any sleep tonight?"

"Not if I don't make it back to the hotel tonight. It wouldn't be the first time." He pushed off the wall and paced. "Baby, I'm going to have to run in a second or I'll be missed."

"Okay. Take care of yourself, now. I'll be dreaming about you."

He knew that wasn't meant to sting, but it did anyway. This whole thing sucked for them both. "Make sure I'm doing something naughty. Miss you."

"I hear you. I promise to make you spin in circles." Sterling's chuckle was husky, a little wry. "Miss you too, honey. Have fun."

"You bet. Night." He ended the call and went back into the suite, finding Lulu sitting right where he'd left her at the bar. Maybe he'd get another cup of coffee. It was going to be a long night.

15

"Happy New Year's Eve, Bit. How goes it?"

Sterling ran a finger down his beer bottle, telling himself not to peel the label off. That was bad luck or some such shit. "It goes."

"Where are you? It's fucking loud. Y'all partying already?"

Not fucking likely. He'd spent the night alone, with Jonas's client needing this and that, and when it was clear his lover was fixin' to be busy for the next few days, he'd just left Jonas a note on the pillow:

Gonna head to the airport and get a flight home. Holler when you can. I love you. I'll call and set up a visit. Don't kiss anybody at midnight. I'll be thinking about you.

"No, man. I'm in the airport having a beer. There's a flight to Phoenix in a few hours that I'm hoping to grab a seat on."

"Hold up. What happened?"

He knew he shouldn't have picked up the damn phone. The last thing he wanted to do right now was talk, even with Chance.

"Bit? Where's Jonas?"

"Working for some dragon lady. There's just no sense me hanging around here when I could be home with Gracie. I ain't mad." Much. And if he was? Jonas had said this wasn't going to be easy.

"Shit, I'm sorry man." Chance sighed into the phone. "You want me to pick you up in Phoenix? I can drive out."

"No. It's a long drive, and what if I can't make the flight? I can either hop a flight into the 'Burque or just rent a car." Sterling smiled, though. Chance was a good, good man. "We'll figure it out."

He hoped.

"Text me when you know what flight you're on, huh? And let me know if you need anything. We'll get a beer when you get in."

"Sounds like a plan, buddy. I have a new foal you might want to meet." He had puppies coming, calves.

"I'm in. Maybe Bobby can join us. You fly safe, champ." Chance didn't draw out the goodbyes any longer and just hung up, leaving his ass alone on a barstool again. But he barely had time to decide that yeah, he was having another beer, before it rang again.

That was a number he recognized, and he shouldn't pick it up either, but what the hell?

"Is this Mister Kingsolver? This is Hank Brooks."

League management. Perfect.

"Howdy, sir. How goes?" *What the fuck do you want, man?* "Happy New Year."

"Oh. Yeah. Happy New Year to you. So, listen. I won't keep you with it being a weekend and all. We were super happy with some of the work you did out East, and we wanted to know what you thought of the experience. What your impressions were of Mister Burke specifically. You have any thoughts for me?"

"He is a class act." The words left his lips immediately, without a single hesitation. "I was totally out of my league, and he had my back."

And I fell in love with him.

"We heard a little about that. Chance Leonards said he was a pretty bright guy too. So you'd recommend him for the future, then? If we needed him?"

"Lord yes. He speaks cowboy now and high-dollar folks and media guys. Seriously, I thought he was something else."

"That's just great. That's what we needed to know. Thanks for your time, Mister Kingsolver. I'll pass that on to the folks that need to know. I'll let you go, and you have a good holiday. Sounds like your party has started already!"

"That's me. Party animal extraordinary." He rolled his eyes at his little joke.

"What else does a cowboy with a million bucks do?" Brooks laughed. "Good night, now." The line went dead.

"He goes to New York City and falls in love."

16

"No. Eight is way too early, Doug. You know Lulu. She's not even going to be awake until noon."

Lulu was notorious for making the rest of creation operate on her schedule. In the past, Jonas had arranged for restaurants to be open at 2:00 a.m. just for her. He'd had breakfast sent up to her room at 2:00 p.m. Lulu's day started when everyone else was having lunch, and she had enough money to get what she wanted, when she wanted it.

This was a magazine spread Doug was calling about, and he knew the guy wasn't thrilled, but Lulu wasn't the only celebrity they'd made accommodations for.

"So... two?"

"Uh-uh. Five."

Doug snorted. "What? *Five*?"

Jonas nodded as if Doug could see him. "Yes." She'd interview until nine and then go to dinner.

"Fine. Can we make it Tuesday, then? I have to make arrangements."

"Tuesday is...." He checked her calendar and added the

appointment. "Yep. Good. Tuesday. I'll send over her green room sheet."

"Oh, goodie." Doug laughed, though, and Jonas laughed back.

"Never a dull moment. Talk to you soon."

He hung up and ducked into his hotel room, finding a smile for Sterling.

"I'm so sorry, baby. I'm back for a few. I've got maybe an hour and...." He looked around the room. "Baby?" He headed for the bathroom. "Sterling?"

He knew Sterling had left him, knew it, and he was halfway into a furious text about exactly how bad Sterling sucked when he found Sterling's note.

I love you.

He sank down onto the bed and read the words again. That wasn't something you said to someone you were leaving.

Shit. He glanced at his phone in a panic, making sure he hadn't hit Send, then breathed and deleted the text.

So they were doing this. This was a shitty way to spend New Year's Eve, though, and that was his fault. Well, his job's fault, but it was his job. And dammit, he'd wanted to say it first, and he'd been about to the other night when Sid fucking called and interrupted them.

Fucking job. He loved it and he hated it, but tonight he hated it a lot more.

He looked back at his phone, changing the tone of his text entirely.

Got your note. It's lame to say on New Year's I guess but I really am sorry.

I love you too. He wasn't going to say it by text. At the very least he'd say it on the phone.

Hey honey. U just getting done? No worries. Work sucks, sitting at the airport having a beer.

He'd asked Sterling to stay, and now the cowboy was alone on New Year's, drinking at an airport bar, and he felt like a first-class asshole. He should have known better. What had he been thinking?

He hadn't been. He'd been high on hormones and falling in love.

He couldn't apologize again. That would be pathetic, but he wasn't ready to cut off the conversation either.

When is your flight?

Don't know. I'll head in @6ish for standby.

Was he supposed to try to talk Sterling out of going? Should he be protesting and begging his lover to stay or something? He felt like he should, but the fact was Sterling knew he'd be out well past midnight, maybe all night long again, and Sterling was scheduled on a plane Sunday already.

New Year's was going to suck for them both.

I don't want to kiss anyone else. I promise.

You got all mine too. A great selfie came next, Sterling making a dipshit kissy face.

God, he missed that face. He hated that it was only as far away as the airport, but they couldn't be together. He grinned and sent a short video back of him blowing a kiss and winking.

How the hell was this fair? Sterling was... *fuck.* He was who Jonas wanted to be with, full stop, and he knew Sterling wanted the same thing.

Sorry, baby. Gotta run. I have to get ready for this damn party.

He stood up and tossed his phone on the bed, but only

got as far as the bathroom door before it started to ring. "Dammit, Lulu. I'm allowed to shower." He walked back over and picked it up, looking at the number. It wasn't Lulu. It was a 720 area code. Where the hell was that?

He tossed the phone back on the bed and went to get in the shower.

As he started the water and got undressed, he tried to let thoughts of Sterling go and focus on work. Lulu needed dinner, he needed to get her in the back door for the party, he wanted to make sure she—

Wait. Did he know anyone in a 720?

It bothered him the whole time he was showering. So much for focusing on work.

There was a voicemail waiting for him when he hopped out. Probably a wrong number, but he took a second to google the area code and figured out it was probably Denver.

Denver?

He put his phone on speaker to listen to the voicemail.

"Mister Burke? This is Hank Brooks with the Western League of Bull Riders. I'd like to give you a holler about a job offer. We're looking for a media specialist to travel with the show, help with local media, Twittering and all. Give me a holler."

Twittering?

Wait, was this for real? He blinked and played the message again. WLBR. Media specialist. Yeah, that was a legit job offer. Twittering and all.

He froze for a second, eyes on his phone. Could he do this? Just pick up and go? Did he want to?

Fuck yeah, he did.

He dialed Hank Brooks back and pulled out his suitcase.

Traveling with the show? That meant he and Sterling would be on the road together. A lot.

The line rang, and he didn't give another thought to the fact that he'd lost his mind.

"Mister Brooks? Happy New Year. This is Jonas Burke returning your call."

S terling sat and waited.

Ten minutes before he had to get in line at security and take his chances on the flight. If he missed it, maybe he could get to Denver or Dallas.

Christ on a crutch, he wanted....

Shit, he couldn't have what he wanted. He wanted Jonas to be close. He wanted that kiss at midnight. He wanted to introduce Jonas to Momma, to Daddy, but mostly to Gracie. Gracie was going to love him.

His phone chimed in his pocket, and he pulled it out, trained to respond to that sound like everyone else was these days.

Got you on a flight to ABQ through Denver.

How? He asked the question before it hit him that his Jonas was the one who'd found him a way to get home.

WLBR has deep pockets. United. Gate A20. Better hurry.

Okay. They have my tickets at the ticket counter??? He grabbed his bag, his hat, and started jogging, grateful as hell he'd paid his tab.

Tickets are waiting for you at the gate.

K

He had a standby ticket, his TSA-Precheck, and beer-fueled adrenaline to get him moving, which was a blessing, because he did hate the take-your-boots-off drama.

New Year's Eve was pretty dead at the airport, and he had the gate in sight in no time. He wished Jonas had told him exactly what time this plane was supposed to take off so he knew what kind of hurry he was actually in. He still had a little hustle left in him when he got there, but he must have swallowed down that last beer too fast, because there was a guy at the check-in counter who he'd have sworn was Jonas.

Then the guy turned toward him and smiled, and there was no question. He'd know that toothy grin anywhere.

"Mister Kingsolver." Jonas nodded to him, still smiling. "Anna was just finding us seats."

About ten thousand things ran through his brain all at the same time, hitting him like a freight train, but 98 percent of them were joyous, so that was okay. It was going to be okay, because his lover cared enough to get that kiss at midnight.

"You get done with your working?"

"So done." Jonas beamed at him, not the fake toothy thing, but genuinely happy. "I quit."

Sterling blinked. Huh. "No shit? Good on you."

Quit. Quit and coming home with him.

"My new job—with the league—starts Monday. A couple of cowboys put in a good word for me. You might know them?" Jonas winked at him. "I do have to travel with the show, but I get things like holidays off and guaranteed vacation."

"You mean.... Really?" What a Christmas present. Please, Jesus, let him be hearing the words that he thought Jonas was saying.

"Well, gentlemen, it's toward the back of the plane, but I managed to get you seated together." The attendant handed them their boarding passes.

"Thank you, Anna. That's fantastic."

"Have a good flight. We'll be boarding in just a few minutes."

Jonas picked up his bag and moved them away from the counter. "I'm just playing with you. Here's the deal. The league called and offered me a job as their on-tour media specialist. You remember you and Chance were talking about it? I guess he said something, and they'd been talking about hiring someone anyway.... I don't know, this guy Hank went on and on, but they want me to do what I was doing for you on the tour. For you still, and also kind of boots on the ground PR for the league too."

They started calling the preboards, and folks were moving all around them.

"The logistics are a little.... Man, I have a lot of balls in the air, but...." Jonas smiled. "I'm with you. I'll figure the rest of it out."

"With me." *Praise God.*

He didn't know how to process this. He didn't understand, but you know what? He didn't have to. Presents were to be accepted with grace and thanks.

Sterling whooped and grabbed Jonas, spinning him around, right there in the airport.

Jonas laughed, the sound pure happiness.

A million dollars and a Jonas with a smile that lit up the world.

Santa had been damn good to him.

THEY'D BEEN HOLDING hands since the plane took off, and Jonas still wasn't ready to let go. Everything felt surreal. He hadn't had five minutes to really think about anything. Taking the job was a no-brainer, but everything else felt so open-ended. It was the right decision, he knew that, but he still had an apartment to deal with in New York, he had a contract to negotiate on Monday with the league, and he'd... he was pretty sure he'd just moved to New Mexico for good.

He was excited, nervous, and absolutely overjoyed.

He told himself it was the beginning of an incredible adventure. He knew pretty much nothing about bull riding, but he was going to learn pretty damn fast. He'd never even been to New Mexico. But that didn't matter. The man he was in love with lived there.

"I keep thinking I ought to pinch myself," Sterling whispered.

Yeah. He knew that feeling. "I keep thinking this is the rightest wrong thing I've ever done."

He knew it would have challenges. He assumed they weren't going to be holding hands when they got off the plane, or pretty much anywhere in public on tour, and it had been a long time since he'd had to be careful. There would still be time apart—maybe more than they'd like. But at least they'd be living in the same universe, and mostly in the same time zone. And this job, he'd been assured, would have plenty of time off.

"I love the idea of knowing you'll be at the events. We'll have a damn ball. We have to get you some boots and jeans."

Boots and jeans. Maybe. He didn't want to be a poser. They'd hired a New Yorker and they knew it. "I'll get to see you ride. How fucking cool is that? And meet Grace and see your place. I'm still trying to get my head around it, but I'm so excited."

Sterling looked down at their joined fingers, inhaled deep, and then let the breath out. "I don't know how to say thank you enough for trusting me."

"Sterling." He lifted his lover's chin to catch those deep, dark eyes. "You're the most genuine man I've ever met. I never had a doubt. My heart just knows. I love you."

"Oh." Sterling beamed at him like he'd hung the moon or held the ladder for the one who did. "Handy, 'cause I love you too."

He squeezed Sterling's hand and looked out the window at the dark sky, wondering where they were. It was funny how now that he'd made the decision he just wanted to get on with it. He didn't want to be on a plane. He wanted to be in Denver. Or in New Mexico. Living the life he'd just taken on.

"I have to stay in Denver until Tuesday night. I've got meetings with management. But we can get you on a flight home tomorrow if you need to get back sooner."

"I'll hang with you. The folks will understand. We can go to the Buckhorn and have a steak, welcome in the New Year."

"I've never been to Denver. Jesus, I've never really been anywhere. This is crazy." He grinned at Sterling. "It is crazy, but I really do love you."

"There's nothing wrong with a little crazy." Sterling leaned close. "And I can't wait to show you the house, the horses." There was a pregnant pause. "Our bed."

He blinked at Sterling, surprised and pleased by those

words. "Ours, hm? I do like the sound of that." He was a little relieved too. He'd invited himself along. He hadn't really asked if he could move in, though that had been implied, so it was good to hear Sterling confirm it so confidently. "'Ours' has a good ring to it."

"Doesn't it? I sent a text home, telling them I would be home with you in time for their cruise. I'll call at midnightish."

"Midnightish their time? New York? How many midnights do we get tonight? We're rewinding the clock here."

"We'll take all three. I'm not above taking advantage." That was a wicked expression, a lewd wink.

"I'm totally in. We deserve all three, for sure." He looked at his watch, which was still set two hours ahead of Denver. "I guess I should take myself off New York time, huh?"

"Home will be Mountain, but you'll be wandering like mad. We do an event in Hawaii, you know...."

"No shit, really?" *Hawaii. Damn.* "This is going to be the best job ever." This could be more than a job, really. It had the potential to become a career, if he played his cards right. "Hawaii. Wow. Where else?"

"This year? New York, Nashville, Orlando, Charleston, Dallas, Houston, Oklahoma City, New Orleans, Atlanta, Seattle, Sao Paolo, Sydney...."

"What? Wait. Sydney?" He looked at Sterling and laughed. "I guess I would have found this out on Monday, but thanks for letting me know. Now I won't faint in the conference room." *So long, Lulu. Not gonna miss you at all.*

"We're going to go everywhere. I am the champ. I'm expected to show. Have you been to Brazil?"

"Baby, I told you. I haven't been fucking *anywhere*. It's all new to me. This is gonna be insane." He should probably be dreading the learning curve, but he was actually inspired by it. He was gonna rock this. He had to. His—

He looked at Sterling. "What do you like better? Lover or boyfriend?"

"Lover." That was immediate and sure. "This ain't no teenage crush. This is love worth leaving everything you know for."

"Yeah? Think I should do that?" If he smiled any harder, he was going to hurt himself.

"I think you have. I think I'm a lucky son of a bitch too."

"Mmm. I might be the lucky one." He looked at his watch again and changed it. "*Home* is Mountain time."

"Yessir. It most definitely is." Sterling's grin was so smug.

Shit, they didn't need jet fuel to keep their plane in the air. He and Sterling were flying without it.

They were both good for conversation, so the four-hour plane ride went by pretty fast, but not nearly fast enough. He'd never wanted off a plane so badly in his life. He wanted to celebrate. Each other, his new job, the New Year—all of it. And strapped into a seat with two inches of legroom and a stranger in the aisle seat wasn't the way to do it.

When they were finally in Denver, they got off the plane and onto the tram, which was almost empty.

"I love the guitar."

Jonas frowned at his lover. "What guit—oh."

The tram played a wicked little riff as it stopped.

"I guess you've been here once or twice?" He winked at Sterling, who'd probably been through here dozens of times. "You know what's weird? I'm on your turf now. I'm following you around."

"I promise to take very good care of you. I won't even make you wear itchy shirts."

He laughed loud enough he felt like he should apologize

to the three other people on the tram with them. "You're so good to me."

"I swear to God." And didn't that sound amazing. Like a promise. Like a real, honest-to-God promise.

Like, maybe a vow.

Jonas nodded to him, hoping the nod and his eyes said enough for now. "Thank you, baby. I promise too." He wanted a kiss. God, it was worse than an itch he couldn't reach. It nagged at him.

"Good deal. Come on. Move your heinie. I need that kiss at midnight."

They got down to the baggage claim, and Sterling caught sight of a man holding a tablet. "Burke. That's you, honey."

Neither of them had more than their carry-ons, so Jonas winked at him and led the way, offering the driver a hand. "Jonas Burke. This is Sterling Kingsolver. Are you our ride?"

"Yes, sir. Car's this way. I got my lady with me, idling close."

"That's handy, thank you." He tossed a grin over his shoulder at Sterling and then followed along. "What's your name?" That was good, right? *Don't be an aloof New Yorker even if you look like one.*

"Carlton. Pleased to meet you. You're going to the Westin?" Carlton smiled at him, the look surprisingly happy.

He shrugged. "If that's what they told you, then yes. Honestly I—oh, wait. I have cell service now." He pulled out his phone and found the email. "Yes, the Westin. Thanks."

"Excellent. We've got time to get there for you to get checked in before next year."

"Hopefully plenty of time for you to get off the clock so you can enjoy midnight with your date too." He shivered as they stepped outside. "Geez, it's just as cold here as it is in New York."

"But it's snowing!" Sterling laughed, face up to the sky.

Look at that. Snowflakes caught in Sterling's stubble, bounced off the battered old hat, and when Sterling stuck his tongue out to catch the flakes, it was Jonas who melted.

"Sorry, let me get you guys out of the weather." Carlton waved, and a black car rolled up to meet them.

"No rush. The snow is beautiful." Just like his man. Inside and out.

"It is. Tomorrow we'll go play in it." Sterling's laugh rang out, filled with crystal-clear joy.

"I can't wait."

Carlton opened the back door. "Hop on in."

"Come on, Frosty, we'll play tomorrow. We have midnight to beat." He tugged on Sterling's sleeve.

"Let's go. Good thing we like hotel rooms, huh?" Sterling followed him into the car, nodding to the lady behind the wheel. "Evenin', ma'am."

"Happy New Year, champ."

Jonas watched her smile at Sterling and tried not to roll his eyes. He knew this would be part of the deal, but he didn't have to play along.

Carlton opened her door and led her around to the passenger side under an umbrella, and while they were both out of the car, Jonas leaned toward Sterling, teasing. "Champ."

"You know it." It shocked the hell out of him when Sterling leaned right in and kissed him. Hard.

He blinked, resisting for a second and then wondering why. If Sterling wasn't concerned, why the hell should he be? He relaxed and let Sterling have him, grabbing the front of the cowboy's coat for balance. Sterling's kiss was so hungry it nearly knocked him over.

"Love you. I ain't stupid, but I ain't ashamed either, okay?"

It didn't get much clearer than that. He blinked again and smiled. "Okay. I love you, and I'm not ashamed at all. But I'm definitely clueless right now, so don't take it personally if I play it safe."

"Of course not. You don't mack at work, right? That's not cool, especially if you work together."

Truth be told, that was what he'd been the most concerned about, and Sterling just made it easy. "Cool, but... did you just say *mack*?" He flashed his teeth and chuckled.

"I did. It's all good." That grin looked wicked as hell.

Carlton took off for the hotel, and he watched the snow out the window reflecting in the streetlights as they drove.

He couldn't see much with the snow, but really all he cared about was what his watch said. "It's already eleven."

"Not to worry, we're almost there." Carlton nodded to him in the rearview mirror.

"We'll be fine. We'll make it. We'll have our kiss." Sterling sounded stubborn.

"Damn right we will." He threaded his fingers into Sterling's. "And maybe a dance?"

"I have music on my phone." Sterling's hand was trembling, just the barest bit.

He wasn't sure he understood what that was about, but he closed his fingers tighter, making sure Sterling felt him. "Perfect."

"I'm gonna pull under the valet area and let y'all out. Keep you out of the snow."

"Thanks, Carlton. That would be great."

He felt like a kid, gawking out the window at the city as

they drove downtown. A few minutes later, they pulled up just where Carlton said. "Ready, cowboy?"

"I have never been more ready in my whole life, honey."

"Me neither." He laughed and climbed out of the car, tugged his bag onto his shoulder, and they headed into the hotel.

18

Sterling just couldn't believe this was real. That they were honest going to....

Breathe.

He grinned at Jonas, who was standing at the registration desk, looking at his watch over and over.

Miracles happened. Love at first sight was real.

Sometimes you just had to give thanks for gifts you were given.

Finally, Jonas held up the key card and grinned.

"Well, come on! Time's a tickin'."

"I know, I know. Bull's in the chute, right?" Jonas laughed at himself. "I really shouldn't try to talk like a cowboy, even if I am going to be hanging out with them. A lot." They bumped shoulders and hurried to the elevators.

"You'll be fine, honey. I have faith in you. Give you a year and you'll be cowboying up on a daily basis." Sterling pushed the Up button and grinned at his lover, feeling himself tingle like he was fixin' to ride. "What floor?"

"Twenty-one. Did you know there is a rooftop pool? It's

heated and it's open in the winter. How cool is that? Too bad my suit is in New York." Jonas backed onto the empty elevator, eyes on him.

"We should go buy some." Could you buy swim trunks in Denver in January?

"Maybe. If we decide we should leave the hotel room tomorrow." Jonas leaned closer as the elevator doors closed. "When was your last New Year's kiss? I haven't had one in... gosh. Four years?"

"Three for me, but this is the first time with someone like you." Someone special and amazing and right.

"Well. Someone like me is going to make sure I get this one. And then I might see if I can convince you I should get the rest of them too."

"I think you're pretty safe on that." Sterling met Jonas's eyes, held the gaze. "You know, this will be the first New Year's Eve kiss with someone I'm in love with."

Jonas touched Sterling's jaw, fingers dragging lightly over his stubble. "I—"

The elevator doors opened on their floor, and Jonas winked at him. "What time is it?"

"Hurry. We have six minutes." They could turn the ball drop on the TV, take off their coats, open the curtains to see the city.

They jogged down the long hall to their room, and were both a little breathless as Jonas keyed in. "You know the local TV channels?"

"Nope. Is there a list?" He tugged off his coat and yanked the curtains open.

Jonas grabbed the remote and turned on the TV, then dropped his coat on the bed. "Uh... ah. Got it. The guy at the desk said we'd be able to see fireworks out the window."

"Window's open." He grinned at Jonas and curled a finger, beckoning him.

"Coming, cowboy. Countdown will be on TV in... two minutes?" Jonas stepped right in close, grabbed his belt, and pulled them together. "Damn. I thought this only happened in fairy tales."

"This can be our fairy tale. I don't mind. Once upon a time there was a rodeo cowboy who met an amazing big-city PR guy that took him to sing karaoke."

"Once upon a time there was a PR guy who met a sweet and studly bull rider that swept him off his feet, took him across the country, and kissed him on a snowy New Year's Eve." Jonas grinned at him. "Oops. Spoilers."

"Not for very much longer, honey. Soon it'll be a great memory." Listen to him, being all romantic and shit.

Jonas leaned on him and looked out the window. "The city is bright in the snow."

"Uh-huh." He couldn't look away from Jonas.

The crowd on the TV got loud. It felt like Jonas was vibrating in his arms. "Countdown! Ten, nine." Jonas looked at him, searching his eyes. "I love you, Sterling."

Seven. Six. "I love you, honey. Swear to God."

Jonas held his eyes, the gaze full of truth and intimacy. "We're going to have a hell of a year."

The fireworks went off, and he pressed his lips to Jonas's, kissing his lover with everything he had. Jonas made a needy sound that was muffled by the contact and gripped his biceps tight, using them for balance.

It wasn't the first kiss, he didn't think for a second that it would be the best, but it was one he would remember when he was old and gray.

They missed most of the fireworks, indulging in their first kiss of the New Year, but when they parted, Jonas's smile was brighter and every bit as beautiful. "Happy New Year!"

Sterling grinned, tracing Jonas's bottom lip. Mr. Teeth. God, Sterling loved him. "Happy New Year, honey."

Jonas fished his phone out of his pocket and waved it at him. "Can I have this dance?"

EPILOGUE

"Oh, man."

It was barely two in the afternoon, and the sky was already getting dark. The snow had started about fifteen minutes ago, and it was still light flakes for now, but the forecast had said they'd be buried by morning.

Jonas made sure the four-wheel drive was on and pointed his truck for home, shaking his head again at the length of the damn driveway. Between Sterling and Jonas's in-laws, the Kingsolvers owned a lot of property out here, and their houses were both pretty far off the road. By the time he parked, it was snowing hard.

He'd told Gracie he'd be home by two, and she was kind of a stickler for being on time, so he grabbed the shopping bags and his phone, tucked his hat down tight on his head, and made a run for it, managing to keep his balance until he hit the porch. He set one foot on the slick boards and skidded, slamming right into the front door.

He might have fallen if two of the biggest, silliest Saint Bernards on earth hadn't been right there with the hottest two-time champion cowboy to catch him. It did not escape him that his puppy, Ring, the dorkiest Aussie on earth, just ran around them all in circles, barking. He laughed and handed Sterling one of the shopping bags.

"Hey there, Bit. Catching snowflakes?" He'd better be careful—Sterling had made it through last season without any major injuries. "Cowboy Knocked Unconscious by Lover" wasn't a headline he wanted to be reading.

"Hey, baby. I was feeding everyone early. Gracie has been watching TV and dusting." Sterling rolled his eyes but grinned. "She loves the dresser you found for her room."

"Yeah?" That made him smile. "That's awesome." He'd found it, fixed it, painted it, and moved it in. "I got us some beer. And I know Gracie isn't a fan of noisemakers and confetti poppers so...." He pulled a colorful bottle out of the bag he was holding. "I got us bubbles for midnight instead."

It was another snowy New Year's Eve.

"You are a good man." Sterling leaned in, kissed him sweet and slow. "The folks are tickled that she can spend the night so they can sleep."

"She asked. She doesn't ask me for much." He liked that she'd asked him. He was really starting to feel like family. "Come on inside. I promised her puzzle time at two when I got back." He shouldered through the front door and held it open for Sterling and the dogs.

Sterling was talking about a fourth. *Oy*.

"Jonas! You are almost late. Do you need help?" Gracie came up to him. "Bubba was mean to me, did he tell you? He made me stay in."

"The weather sucks, Sister. You know that." Sterling rolled his eyes dramatically, but Jonas knew Sterling adored his sister.

"I slid across the porch. I'd have landed on my keister if not for Lucy and Sebastian. Good thing they're big. Did you pick a new puzzle?" He handed her the bubbles and then ducked into the kitchen to put away the munchies for later and stick the beer in the fridge.

He could hear Gracie squealing happily over the bubbles, the TV playing in the background. It was so weird and normal, all at once—he'd been on vacation since Thanksgiving, and he had another week left after today. He had a house. Dogs. Horses, for God's sake.

It was everything he'd imagined. Everything he wanted. No kids yet, but they weren't ready for that anyway. One of them was going to have to be home more often before they could do that, and he assumed Sterling had a run at a third championship in mind.

He stopped as he left the kitchen and watched Sterling goofing with Lucy. There was a puzzle out on the dining room table, and he made his way over to see what Grace had picked out. "Butterflies, Grace? This is going to be a tough one."

"I know, but they're so pretty. Are we going to have a fire, Bubba?"

"Whenever y'all want." Sterling looked over at him, eyes dragging over him like they had a year ago.

"Wait till dark, maybe?" They weren't in a rush this year, but he'd bet they'd make their own fireworks. "You can pick the music again."

"Are you going to kiss your fiancé at midnight, Bubba?" Grace asked.

He grinned, and he could feel the heaviness of his ring. He'd never forget sitting at Sterling's folks' having Thanksgiving dinner when his lover got down on one knee.

"I most certainly am, Sister."

Jonas laughed. "Damn right you are."

Sterling's ask was a surprise, but his yes didn't take any

thought at all. He'd already booked every midnight kiss with Sterling from now until eternity. New Year's or otherwise. The ring just made it known to the world.

"Good." Gracie opened the puzzle box and poured the pieces out on the table. "Let's do this."

Their second New Year's Eve together, their second snowed-in New Year's Day. It was like the universe was reminding him he wasn't going anywhere.

Like he needed the reminder.

Jonas smiled at Sterling as he pulled up a chair.

"You're on, Gracie. Your brother and I have solved way harder puzzles than this one." He leaned down and gave his fiancé a quick, hard kiss. "Right?"

Sterling nodded to him, music filling the air. "Yessir. We have. Together."

Interested in learning more about BA's cowboys and Jodi's gentlemen? Want free fiction and news? Join our newsletters!

What's Up with Jodi
http://bit.ly/whatsupjodi

Spurs and Shifters
https://lp.constantcontact.com/su/A9CRUzp/baandjulia

WRECKED
Jodi Payne and BA Tortuga

The call comes when Beckett Adler least expects it. He's made a new life for himself in Vermont and has a law practice of his own. After four years he's even stopped wearing his wedding ring. So when he finds out his husband, bull rider Skyler Paulson, has been seriously injured at an event, he isn't sure what he wants to do. He knows what's right though, so he heads down to Baltimore to bring his man home.

Sky knows his injuries are a career-ender, and he can't believe Beck has come for him after all this time. He's not a hundred percent sure what went wrong with their marriage and he has no idea how to be anything but a bull rider. But he wants this second chance, so he grabs at it with both hands.

There's a lot Sky has to learn, from how to walk again to how to settle down with the man he loves. Beck needs to learn to open up and how to be more trusting. For their marriage to work again, both men will have to find a way to meet in the middle. Because neither of them wants to be wrecked anymore.

Read More Here

Happy Holidays, Y'all!

We want to thank you for giving Window Dressing a try. We hope you enjoyed the story.

If you can spare a few minutes to post a review at the retail website where you made your purchase, we'd very much appreciate it!

Don't forget to "like" our Facebook pages and groups to keep up with all the news--new releases, sales announcements, giveaways, sneak peeks-- and of course the rodeo pictures, coffee memes and just general fun. We'd love to have all y'all!

Yeehaw and thanks for reading!

BA & Jodi

ABOUT JODI

JODI takes herself way too seriously and has been known to randomly break out in song. Her men are imperfect but genuine, stubborn but likable, often kinky, and frequently their own worst enemies. They are characters you can't help but fall in love with while they stumble along the path to their happily ever after. For those looking to get on her good side, Jodi's addictions include nonfat lattes, Malbec and tequila any way you pour it.

Website: jodipayne.net
Newsletter: What's Up with Jodi?
All Jodi's Social Links: linktr.ee/jodipayne

ABOUT BA

Texan to the bone and an unrepentant Daddy's Girl, BA Tortuga spends her days with her basset hounds, getting tattooed, texting her grandbabies, and eating Mexican food. When she's not doing that, she's writing. She spends her days off watching rodeo, knitting and surfing Pinterest in the name of research. BA's personal saviors include her wife, Julia Talbot, her best friends, and coffee. Lots of coffee. Really good coffee.

Having written everything from fist-fighting rednecks to hard-core cowboys to werewolves, BA does her damnedest to tell the stories of her heart, which was raised in Northeast Texas, but has heard the call of the high desert and lives in the Sandias. With books ranging from hard-hitting GLBT romance, to fiery ménages, to the most traditional of love stories, BA refuses to be pigeon-holed by anyone but the voices in her head.

BA loves to talk to her readers and can be found at http://batortuga.com/ and her newsletter signup link is http://bit.ly/BAJulianews

AVAILABLE FROM JODI & BA

East Meets Westerns

(single titles)

Heart of a Redneck

Wrecked

Land of Enchantment

Window Dressing

Flying Blind

Special Delivery, A Wrecked Holiday Novel

Keeping Promises

The Cowboy and the Dom Trilogy

First Rodeo, Book One

Razor's Edge, Book Two

No Ghosts, Book Three

The Soldier and the Angel, a Cowboy and Dom Novel

The Triskelion Series

Breaking the Rules

Les's Bar Series

Just Dex, Book One

The Lone Star Series

Tending Tyler, Book One

The Collaborations Series